"The truth is, I've discovered something for which I feel more passion than racing," Ramon announced in a firm voice.

"Hard to believe, is it not? Racing has been my life for over a decade, but with my brother so happily married and starting his family I find I can't wait to enjoy the same. I'm deeply in love and, well…"

He moved around Isidora so he was no longer behind the podium and sank to one knee beside her.

A massive gasp went through the crowd.

The cacophony of flashes and clicks increased, but the shouting of questions ceased. An eerie expectancy characterized the wordless explosion of repeated shutter-click-flash. The lights strobed against his skin as he looked up at Isidora's incredulous expression.

She paled as comprehension dawned. Her eyes showed white around her gray irises. One hand came to her mouth and she might have said, "Don't you dare."

"You ... ne. So, *n* happ

The Sauveterre Siblings

Meet the world's most renowned family…

Angelique, Henri, Ramon and Trella—two sets
of twins born to a wealthy French tycoon and his
Spanish aristocrat wife. Fame, notoriety and an
excess of bodyguards is the price of being part of
their illustrious dynasty. And wherever the Sauveterre
twins go, scandal is sure to follow!

They're protected by the best security money can
buy—no one can break through their barriers… But
what happens when each of these Sauveterre siblings
meets the one person who can breach their heart…?

Meet the heirs to the Sauveterre fortune
in Dani Collins's fabulous new quartet:

Pursued by the Desert Prince

His Mistress with Two Secrets

Bound by the Millionaire's Ring

Available now!

And look for

Trella and Prince Xavier's story

Coming soon!

BOUND BY THE MILLIONAIRE'S RING

BY
DANI COLLINS

MILLS & BOON

First Published in Great Britain 2017
By Mills & Boon, an imprint of HarperCollins*Publishers*
1 London Bridge Street, London, SE1 9GF

© 2017 Dani Collins

ISBN: 978-0-263-92479-4

Printed and bound in Spain
by CPI, Barcelona

Canadian **Dani Collins** knew in high school that she wanted to write romance for a living. Twenty-five years later, after marrying her high school sweetheart, having two kids with him, working at several generic office jobs and submitting countless manuscripts, she got The Call. Her first Mills & Boon novel won the Reviewers' Choice Award for Best First in Series from *RT Book Reviews*. She now works in her own office, writing romance.

Books by Dani Collins

Mills & Boon Modern Romance

The Secret Beneath the Veil
Bought by Her Italian Boss
Vows of Revenge
Seduced into the Greek's World
The Russian's Acquisition
An Heir to Bind Them
A Debt Paid in Passion
More than a Convenient Marriage?

The Secret Billionaires

Xenakis's Convenient Bride

The Sauveterre Siblings

Pursued by the Desert Prince
His Mistress with Two Secrets

The Wrong Heirs

The Marriage He Must Keep
The Consequence He Must Claim

Seven Sexy Sins

The Sheikh's Sinful Seduction

The 21st Century Gentleman's Club

The Ultimate Seduction

Visit the Author Profile page
at millsandboon.co.uk for more titles.

Dear Reader, for being such a passionate,
wonderful fan of romance.

CHAPTER ONE

ISIDORA GARCIA DIDN'T glance up as her boss entered her office. She recognized him in her periphery and was only a little surprised he was here in Paris. He was a new father, but when there was a crisis with one of his sisters, particularly Trella, he waded in without hesitation.

"I just saw it," she assured him. "I'm emailing—"

She cut herself off as preternatural knowledge struck. Her body tingled and her skin felt stroked. Her fingers became clumsy while her blood grew hot and thick in her veins.

She didn't have to look up to know that was not Henri Sauveterre advancing on her. It was his twin, Ramon.

A flash of intense vulnerability went through her. Treachery. Anguish.

She clamped down on the rush of emotion, hiding it behind a falsely cool lift of her gaze to the man who looked identical to the one who had arm-twisted her into taking this position. They were both ruthless in their own way, but at least Henri wasn't cruel.

"I didn't know you were in Paris." Her voice came out steady enough to hide the tightness that invaded her throat.

Like Henri, Ramon's dark hair was cut short, but had a tendency to spike on top. His clean-shaven, spectacularly handsome features were sophisticated without being pretty, angular without being rugged. His Sauveterre eyes were green when they were amused and gray when they were not.

His irises were somewhere between slate and ash this morning, making a knot of tension coil in the pit of her stomach. His sensuous mouth sat in a flat line. His honed physique flexed beneath his tailored suit as he set his hands on her desk, leaning in to confront her.

"Why aren't you doing your job?"

His lethal tone cut her in half, sending a burst of adrenaline through her.

Oh, she hated herself for still being sensitive to his every word. Him, with his superiority, and opportunistic streak, and complete lack of conscience. She wanted to hate him. Did hate him. But she remained susceptible. In fact, it was worse, now that she knew how brutal he could be. At least when she'd been young and stupid, she hadn't feared him.

She took a firm grip on herself and tried to hide her dread by casually looking back at her screen. She couldn't absorb what she'd been writing. She waved at her keyboard, aiming for nonchalance. "I'm doing it now. If you weren't interrupting me, I could get on with it."

She managed to sound composed and begged her hand to stay steady. She didn't want to reveal the fine trembles that worked upward from a deep, inner flutter in the pit of her stomach.

Because even with hatred and fear gripping her, she found him utterly compelling.

"What can you possibly do at this stage?" he growled. "The cat is out. Why didn't you prevent it?"

"Prevent your sister's pregnancy?" Her pulse hammered once, hard, as she met his gaze, but she managed to tilt her mouth into a facetious smirk. "Not in my bailiwick, if you can believe it. I've had three discussions with her, suggesting we leak the news in a controlled way. She chose to stay mum."

Pun not intended. Trella was tall and a wizard with cutting cloth to create the effect she wanted, but she was five months along. She couldn't hide it forever.

"You should have had a fourth discussion. And a fifth. Your father had the contacts to keep these things under wraps. Why don't you?"

Her heart stalled. Oh, he was not going to bring her parents into this, was he? That was *such* dangerous ground.

At least it flipped her out of defensive mode into a willingness to go toe-to-toe.

"Even my father can't control every person with a social media account. The photo was posted by a woman visiting her mother at the hospital. You took Trella there yourself—in that car everyone notices. Of course people watched to see who got out."

She punctuated with a look that said, "Take some responsibility for a change."

"The only reason it took this long for the trolls to call it a baby bump was because they were having so much fun shaming her for gaining a few pounds." Then, as she remembered his sister-in-law had delivered twins by emergency cesarean a few days ago, she asked, "How are Cinnia and the babies?"

"Fine." He pushed off the desk, expression blanking to aloofness—it was the way he and all his siblings reacted when questioned about their family, even when the inquiry was sincere.

The Sauveterre twins had become media sensations the minute the second pair, Angelique and Trella, came along. Born to a French tycoon and his Spanish aristocrat wife, the children had been mesmerizing in their mirrored resemblance and elegantly perfect lives.

Then, when the girls were nine, Trella had been kidnapped. She was recovered five days later, but rather than give the family breathing space, the media's microscope had focused even more intently on their slightest move. The pressure had sent their father into an early grave and the fallout had continued for years.

Angelique—Gili to her family—seemed to have found some happiness, though. She was secretly engaged to her soul mate, Kasim, which was why the family had convened in Spain.

Their celebration had been cut short when Cinnia was rushed to hospital.

Trella had jumped into Ramon's distinctive Bugatti Veyron to chase the ambulance with him. Not content with the limited edition Pur Sang, worth millions, Ramon had had one custom-built to his own specifications. It was fully carbon this and titanium that, didn't have a lick of exterior paint and topped out at a speed of over four hundred kilometers an hour.

Isidora was dying to ask if it had air-conditioning.

Worried for Cinnia, Trella had leaped out of the car without taking due care over how much midsection she showed.

Any casual snap of a Sauveterre went viral. And one that allowed the public to speculate on a secret pregnancy and the identity of the father…? There was no containing such a nuclear bomb.

Isidora knew all this because she had grown up with the girls. Her father had worked for Monsieur Sauveterre. She'd had tea parties with the girls before Trella was taken and still had slumber parties with them. She cared deeply for them and wanted the best for the whole family.

That was why Henri had hired her. He trusted her with his sisters and all of the family's most delicate PR announcements—most recently a statement that he and Cinnia had spoken their wedding vows in the hospital with their newborn daughters in attendance.

None of that mattered to Ramon, however. To him, she was an outsider, not entitled to anything more than criticism and a pat. *Fine*.

Fine. It didn't hurt. She was so past yearning for his positive regard.

"I was hoping you were Henri." For a million reasons. "I was going to suggest taking the family portrait with Cinnia and the babies sooner than planned. I'm inundated with requests. Releasing photos might divert this focus on Trella."

"By all means, let's make sacrifices of my brother's innocent children before they're a week old."

She was only trying to help. Swallowing back a lump that formed behind her breastbone, she rose to walk a file to the cabinet in the corner, mostly as an excuse to put distance between them. "Do you have another suggestion?"

"Yes."

Oh, that supercilious attitude grated. If her father hadn't badgered and cajoled, if Henri hadn't offered her disgusting amounts of money, if she didn't adore Trella and Angelique and now Cinnia, and want to protect her friends as much as Henri did, she would quit this job. Even this little bit of interaction with Ramon was too much.

"I'm all ears," she said without turning around. She shoved the file into the cabinet, feeling a burning sensation streak down her back. He was *not* looking at her butt and she was *not* wishing he would. Seriously. She consciously tried not to tense, but she needed to resist him. She was so *done* with this man!

"Arrange a press conference," he said. "I'm announcing my retirement from racing."

Isidora had the nicest ass he'd ever seen—and he was a connoisseur.

When she turned with surprise, one arm remaining atop the filing cabinet so her buttons strained across her breasts, he stole an appreciative glance at that, too, before lifting his gaze to her astonished expression.

Auburn brows framed warm brown eyes. Her gold-tipped lashes were thick and lush. Her glossy hair, which had toned down from a bright copper as a child to a rich burgundy wine, was pulled back in a clip. He couldn't help imagining it falling freely around those high, honey-toned cheekbones. She wore little makeup, needing nothing to give her skin that glow of health, or shape her plump lips.

He typically stuck with overt beauties, ones made with a generous hand that exuded sexuality. When it came to physical companionship, he preferred obvious women and uncomplicated encounters. Indifference was his goal. He didn't objectify women, but they objectified him. He was fine with being trophy-hunted. He gave as much pleasure as he took and they both walked away unharmed and completely satisfied.

Isidora had never offered anything so simplistic. Her years of doe-eyed hero worship had reflected yearnings and expectations he could never fulfill. So he had done her an enormous favor five years ago. He had let her believe he had slept with her mother. That adolescent crush of hers had needed to be crushed.

She still hated his guts for it. Overnight, she had stopped accompanying her father to the office or Ramon's races. She continued to visit his sisters, but sent regrets to any parties the Sauveterres invited her to attend. While completing her degree in public relations, she had maximized work-abroad opportunities. On the few occasions Ramon had crossed paths with her, she had left the room as quickly as she politely could.

That's how he'd made such a study of her ass.

Her contempt had finally gotten to him last year, when he'd seen her at her father's sixty-fifth birthday party. He had rivalries in business and on the track, but no one outright hated him. Isidora had been all grown up, incandescent in a sapphire-blue dress. Surely she was far enough past her childish infatuation to hear the truth and get over her anger.

"I want to bury the hatchet," he had said when he'd cornered her into a waltz. "Let's go somewhere private, talk this out."

"Is that what you're calling it these days? Burying the hatchet?" Her tone had been glacial. "No, thanks." She had walked away before the song finished.

Still acting like a child, he had deduced, but he had her attention now.

"You're retiring," she repeated now, with disbelief. "From racing."

"Si." It was the least he could do for his family.

"But you're still winning. Your fans will be devastated."

"I have sufficient fame and money."

"But… You love it. Don't you?" She closed the file cabinet and faced him, weight hitched to one hip so her knee peeked out the slit in her skirt.

Definitely no longer a child, his libido took great care to note.

"It's just a pastime." Psychologists would say his need for speed was compensation for failing to catch up to Trella when she'd been kidnapped. That might have been true in the beginning, but he was genuinely fascinated by the mechanics of high-performance engines and loved competing. Nevertheless… "This is something I've been considering for some time. I'll continue to sponsor my team and stay involved that way." These were the pat answers he would give the press this afternoon.

"It seems extreme. Trella's pregnancy can't be denied. Not forever."

He folded his arms, not used to defending his decisions to anyone. He didn't bother to soften the condescension in his tone as he explained, "I'm choosing to announce it now to distract from the rumors about her, but quitting racing was inevitable once Cinnia turned up pregnant. Henri can't travel as much as he used to."

He and Henri jointly ran Sauveterre International, but work had been Henri's sport of choice for mental distraction. Ramon had never shirked his responsibilities, but he had never felt guilty handing something to his brother if he had to race.

Henri had greater concerns now. Ramon was more than willing to pick up the slack so his brother could look after his young family.

"So you've been planning this all along?"

"I knew once the babies came, my role would change."

"We all knew you were taking over this office so Henri could move to Madrid, but I don't think anyone expected you to quit racing."

"We planned to make all the announcements next month. With the babies coming early, we've moved up the timetable. I will begin restructuring today. Starting with you."

Her eyes widened. "Me? I arranged a transfer to Madrid. It takes effect with Cinnia's due date, but— Are you saying that with the babies coming early, I need to move that up?"

"You're staying here." He probably shouldn't take so much pleasure in making that statement, but he found enormous satisfaction in it. "My sisters came to Paris with me. They're sorting things at Maison des Jumeaux in preparation for Angelique leaving. Her engagement will be announced soon and there are details with Kasim's family that need your delicate touch."

Isidora's jaw dropped behind her sealed lips, making her cheeks go hollow. Her thick lashes quickly swept down to disguise what might have been a flash of…fear? No. Fury? Why? He wasn't being sarcastic about her delicate touch. She was very good at her job or she wouldn't have the position she held.

He wasn't in the habit of giving anyone ego strokes, however, so he simply continued. "With Trella in the hot seat again, I'll do my best to draw fire with the retirement announcement, but you'll have to manage all of that, as well as the press releases on the restructuring."

"I can do that remotely." She folded her arms, posture stiff and defensive, face turned to the window, where vertical blinds held out most of the July sun along with the building's excellent view of the Seine. "I'll speak to Henri—"

"He just brought home *twins*, Isidora. He's working as little as possible and mostly from home so he can enjoy his children and support his wife. Henri is not your employer, *we* are. We speak for each other and this is something we decided together."

"You decided between you to deny my transfer? Without discussing it with me?"

"Yes." It hadn't even been a discussion. As often happened, Henri had voiced what Ramon had already been thinking. "It's a matter of response time. *Some* of your work can be done remotely, but when a crisis arises, like today's, we need you on the spot to defuse it."

Her mouth tightened. He could see her wheels turning, searching for an alternative. He knew why she was acting like this and he was losing patience with it.

"Perhaps we could coax your father out of retirement?" he said facetiously.

"Don't think I'm not tempted."

"Stow your grudge, Isidora. You're a professional. Act like one."

She lifted haughty brows. "It's not *my* ability to keep things professional that I'm worried about."

"If I was the least bit interested in frostbite below the belt, you'd have something to worry about. I'm not."

He always hit back. *Always.* It came from never wanting to be a victim again.

But when her nostrils pinched and she sniffed like she'd taken a hard jab to her slender middle, he felt a pang of conscience. A shadow of hurt might have flickered in her eyes, but she moved behind her desk, ducking her head and sliding a nonexistent tendril of hair behind her ear, the screen of her hand hiding her expression from him.

When she lifted her face again, it was flushed, but her expression was one of resolve. "I'll hand in my resignation by the end of the day."

The floor seemed to lurch beneath his feet. Her antipathy ran that deep?

As he searched her gaze, unable to believe she was serious, her pupils expanded until her eyes were like black pansies, velvety. Yet disillusioned and empty.

For one heartbeat, the world around him faded. A quiet agony that lived inside him, one he ignored so completely he barely knew it existed, seared to life, flashing such acute pain through him that his breath stalled. Fire, hot and pointed, lit behind his breastbone.

He slammed the door on that dark, tangled, livid place, refusing to wonder how she had managed to touch it by doing nothing but trying to retreat from him.

Why would she even suggest it? The job she held, as someone still fresh from school and not yet twenty-four, was unprecedented. Nepotism had played a part, sure, but she brought a rare and valuable quality to the position: trustworthiness.

Ramon would not be the reason his sisters lost a precious ally.

He wasn't a man who begged, however. Racetracks were not conquered by being nice. She already hated him so there was no point in trying to charm her. Meanwhile, that strange split second of confused feelings left him with the scent of danger in his nostrils. It fueled his need to control. To dominate. To conquer.

He came down on her with the same lack of mercy he showed anyone else who might threaten him or his family.

"*Cariño*, let me explain what will happen if you resign." He moved to lean on her desk again.

She was standing now, blinking with wariness. She stiffened, but she didn't fall back.

He caught a light scent off her skin, something natural and spicy with an intriguingly sweet undertone. Herbs and wildflowers? The base, primitive animal inside him longed to get closer and find out.

Perhaps he would get the chance, he thought darkly, as he continued.

"I know you've signed confidentiality agreements, but given your antagonism toward me, I don't trust you not to take what you know about us to the highest bidder. I will make your life extremely difficult if you walk out of here. There won't be other jobs available to you. Not at this level."

A renewed flush of color swept across her cheekbones. "If that's your way of trying to make me warm up to you, 'hash-tag friendship fail.'"

"Prove your loyalty to our family. Do what we pay you very well to do."

"Me." She pointed at her sternum. "You want *me* to prove *my* loyalty to *your* family."

"Yes. And quit editorializing on mine." He ignored a stab of compunction. "You know *nothing* about my capacity for loyalty or anything else."

"I know what I need to know," she assured him bitterly. "But if you're going to make threats against my career, fine. I'll take the high road and show you what loyalty really is. I'll stay because I care about your sisters and because my father *would* come out of retirement if I quit. His devotion to your family is that ingrained. I never told him that you slept with his wife or he might feel differently. And don't say they were divorced!"

She jabbed her finger at him.

He narrowed his eyes, warning her she was standing on the line.

"It would gut him to know what you did and unlike you, I'm not someone who enjoys making other people miserable."

"I said 'difficult,' *hermosa*. If you want me to make your life miserable, I can arrange that quite easily."

"Job done, *hermoso*," she said with a smile that went nowhere near her eyes. "Will you excuse me? I have a press conference to arrange."

"Isidora," he said gently, without moving. His eyes clashed with her gaze in a way that kept his muscles tight and his skin tingling with exaltation in the battle. "*I* care about my sisters and your father. That's why I'm allowing you to continue with us, and not firing your ass for insubordination. Mind your manners, or you will discover *exactly* what kind of man I am."

CHAPTER TWO

WITH FURY BURNING a hole in the pit of her stomach, Isidora did her job and sent out the notices that a press conference would be held in the media room of Sauveterre International's Paris tower. The skyscraper in Madrid was its twin, built the same year on the same specifications. Until today, Ramon had worked out of that office, which was why she had not requested a transfer back to her home country, where she could be closer to her parents.

She desperately wanted to call her father with the news that Ramon was retiring. Her father had been a fan of all types of racing long before his client's son had begun entering grand prix races at a mere nineteen years. After showing some talent for racing while learning evasive driving, Ramon had spent an inheritance from one of his grandparents on a car and team, much to the late Monsieur Sauveterre's dismay. Ramon had won that first year and had won or placed in nearly every race since.

Some of Isidora's most cherished memories involved catering to her father as he parked himself in front of the television for a twenty-four-hour endurance race, or biting her nails alongside him as cars zoomed through the narrow streets of Monaco. In the beginning, she hadn't been so much a fan of racing as she was of her father's passion and delight in having a companion while he watched.

Of course, by the time she was twelve, she had definitely been a fan of one particular driver, heart pitter-patting as Ramon rocketed through turns and occasionally spun out only to straighten and take over the lead once again.

Ramon's winning streak, coupled with his Sauveterre name and the fact he represented both France and Spain, made him more than a darling in the racing world. It set him on a level beyond infamous. Demigod.

He had certainly dazzled her young heart.

But after That Day, which had actually been an early morning, when she had bumped in to Ramon leaving her mother's house wearing rumpled clothes, a night's stubble and a complete lack of remorse, she had stopped watching the races with her father. She had claimed she was too busy with university, and would go to her deathbed before she admitted she had watched alone, in dorm rooms, or plugged into her laptop, tucked away in a solitary corner of the library.

She hated Ramon Sauveterre, but she had always needed to know he survived to race another day. How could she be disappointed on his behalf that he was giving it up? She ought to be doing a happy dance that he wasn't getting what he wanted for a change, the arrogant, heartless tyrant.

Her father would be even more devastated, but as the former VP of PR for Sauveterre International, he would understand. Even she had understood, before embarking on this profession, that when it came to publicity, Ramon stole the lion's share of attention as a way to take the fall for his family, particularly his sisters.

That behavior had continued even as she'd taken over her father's position. Since she had come aboard earlier this year, she had watched it happen—if somewhat mysteriously. Ramon had to be the source of the leaks, but he took care of them in his own way, never involving her and never charging into her office to demand why she wasn't preventing *his* scandals from going viral.

Still, his escapades always seemed to hit the light at the right time to pull attention from his siblings. When Angelique had been called a two-timer because photos of her kissing not one, but *two* different princes had turned up, photos from one of Ramon's "private" parties had surfaced. He had been half-naked and canoodling with a stripper on each knee. When Trella reentered society via the wedding of a family friend, causing a social-media riot, a tape of Ramon's blue-streaked voice mails had taken over the talk-show circuit. The minute Cinnia's twin pregnancy had become a target, an online feud had erupted between Ramon and a fellow driver.

So, in a way, she wasn't surprised he was announcing his retirement when a secret as big as Trella's pregnancy was hitting the airwaves. It just made Isidora...sad. And sheepish, for calling him faithless.

Not that she would admit that after he had threatened her job and future, the power-drunk bastard. Why did he have to be so hard on her? What had she ever done except like him a little too much?

She smoothed her hair, painted her lips a demure pink and told her throat to stop feeling so raw at the injustice.

She texted Ramon that she would wait for him at the elevator, but Etienne joined her first. He had been her father's protégé and had taken her out a few times last year, breaking it off when their sex life hadn't progressed as he had desired. She had gone to London to finish her degree and had been quite happy to never cross paths with him again.

Then her father had retired and Henri had used a

press-gang of euros and guilt trips to bring her aboard. Etienne had believed he was a shoe-in for her father's position. Instead he had wound up answering to *her*. He was *not* happy.

"So it's true?" he said, his tone bordering on belligerence.

"What's that?"

"Trella is pregnant?" His tone rang with *obviously*. "That's what this press conference is about, isn't it?"

"I'm need-to-know, same as you." She pretended to read something on her phone. "But today's announcement is on another topic entirely."

A beat of silence, then he asked, "You're not going to tell me what that topic is?"

"You'll find out in five minutes. That's why I invited you to hear it firsthand."

He swore, muttering something about favoritism.

When she made no response, he said, "So you don't deny it?"

"Deny what?"

His jaw clenched, then he spat out what had clearly been chewing at him. "You were hired because of your father. You're not even qualified. You don't have my experience."

"I was given a chance because of him, yes. But if I stuff things up, I can assure you they will have no qualms about letting me go."

A door closed down the hall and they went silent as Ramon's firm steps approached. She pasted on the same composed smile she would use to introduce him to the rabid hounds of the press.

"Henri." Etienne greeted Ramon with a deferential nod. He waved at the elevator she'd been holding, inviting Ramon to enter ahead of him.

"Ramon," he amended as he stepped into the car.

"Of course," Etienne said, visibly flustered as he came in last and pressed the button for the bottom floor. "The memo didn't specify." He sent a malevolent look at Isidora. "I didn't realize you were here. I suppose your brother is still in Spain with—"

"Bernardo never had a problem telling us apart," Ramon interjected. "And neither does Isidora. It's a quality we appreciate in those closest to us. Don't ever gossip about my family again. I have no qualms about letting *you* go for *that*."

It wasn't working. After a brief ripple of flashes and murmurs over his announcement, the callouts quickly turned to Trella.

"Can you confirm the pregnancy?"

"When is she due?"

"Who is the father?"

"Ladies and gentlemen, please confine your questions to today's topic." Isidora leaned her fragrant hair under his nose so the microphone picked up her well-modulated voice. "Ramon is retiring from racing to free up his time to restructure the company. These are details that will be of interest to your financial and market readers as well as the sports fans."

Such a smooth, unruffled command as she stayed on message, just like her father. As competent as she was, however, Etienne was right. She lacked experience. She didn't have Ramon's well-honed skill for manipulating the press—techniques he had learned from her father under the worst possible tutelage.

"Cuánto lo siento," Bernardo had said fifteen years ago, pleading for Angelique's forgiveness while Ramon had held her small, sweaty palm in his equally clammy hand.

The police thought a public plea for help would urge people to come forward with tips that could rescue their sister from her kidnappers.

"Emotions move people, Angelique," Bernardo had said. "I don't mean to cause you more pain. *Lo siento mucho.* I know you're frightened and hurting, but please don't try to hide your tears. People need to see how you are feeling. This is what makes it stick in their minds and moves them to act the way we need them to. *Lo lamento mucho.* I wish I didn't have to ask this of you, but I need you to reveal your heart to the camera."

It had been a disgusting thing to ask of a nine-year-old girl. Using her terror and anguish had bordered on exploitation. Their father hadn't been able to watch, too filled with self-contempt at putting his shy, sensitive daughter through such an ordeal when she was already so traumatized. But they had been desperate, all of them.

Their father had held their weeping mother in the other room while Henri stood beside the camera, so Angelique could look at him as she pleaded for Trella's return. Henri had worn the same ravaged expression that Ramon had felt upon his own face.

They had all developed a deep, deep hatred of the public attention that had never been invited and had turned their family into a target in the first place.

After Trella was rescued, and they were trying to move on with their lives, they had all found different ways of coping with the continued attention. Henri stonewalled at every opportunity. Angelique accepted and ignored. Trella had retreated to seclusion, becoming an elusive unicorn who had gone several years without being photographed.

Ramon preferred to play them at their own game. He didn't care what was printed about him. It amused him when the facts were wrong, especially when those "facts" came from him. One of his fellow racers had gleefully exchanged a volley of insults with him for several weeks earlier this summer, to take the pressure off Cinnia as she floundered under the weight of two babies and more attention than anyone should have to suffer—especially if they hadn't become inured to it the way the rest of his family had.

Now another baby was on the way. Ramon would quietly strangle his sister at some point for getting herself into that situation, but that was a job for another day.

Today's task was to protect that unborn Sauveterre. And Trella. Despite the progress she had made in the last year, she was still very fragile. She had barely survived her kidnapping. The critical press that had dogged her for years after had made every effort to finish her off. Ramon was very cognizant that a renewal of that harsh focus could give her a setback.

"Is it true that Trella watched some of your races last year, by pretending she was Angelique?"

Yes, and that was a can of worms that needed to stay closed. Ramon *had* to bring the focus back to him. Leaving racing wasn't doing the job. The dry topic of restructuring a corporation was certainly not holding anyone's attention.

Emotions move people. Reveal your heart to the camera...

His mind raced to find and evaluate options, quickly discovering the line he would have to follow if he wanted to stay in front of the pack.

"The truth is, I've discovered something for which I feel more passion than racing," he announced in a firm voice. "Hard to believe, is it not? Racing has been my life for over a decade, but with my brother so happily married and starting his family, I find I can't wait to enjoy the same. I'm deeply in love and…well—"

He moved around Isidora so he was no longer behind the podium and sank to one knee beside her.

A massive gasp went through the crowd.

The bombardment of flashes and clicks increased, but the shouting of questions ceased. An eerie expectancy characterized that wordless explosion of repeated shutter clicks and flashes. The lights strobed against her skin as he looked up to Isidora's incredulous expression.

She paled as comprehension dawned. Her eyes showed white around her gray irises. One hand came to her mouth and she might have said, "Don't you dare."

"Lo siento, mi amor," Ramon said with loud pride over the mechanical clicks and pops. "I cannot sneak around any longer, trying to keep this quiet. I love you too much."

He couldn't recall ever saying those words to anyone except his mother and siblings. It felt strange, pulling disturbingly at that inner door he kept so firmly closed. The push-pull gave his voice the appropriate amount of unsteadiness as he continued.

"You said if I quit racing, you would marry me. So, *mi corazón. Now* will you make me the happiest man on earth? Our fathers would approve, you know they would." He added the last as a reminder of where her loyalty should lie.

He had to give it to her. She had studied well under Bernardo. Her eyes filled with glossy tears and she didn't try to hide them. Her fingers against her lips trembled. Her other hand was cold when he took it in his, her fingers lax with shock.

The white fingers against her mouth curled into a fist.

"Was that yes?" He pretended he had heard a response no one else could and leaped to his feet. As he crushed her to his front, he played up the joyful act as he exclaimed, "She said yes!"

Then he dug his fingers into her hair, tipped back her head and kissed her.

She stiffened. Her breasts crushed into his chest as she sucked in a shocked breath.

He closed his grip on her more firmly, subtly, but implacably. *Do this*, he urged, but even he had his limits when it came to cold-bloodedly achieving his goals. Rather than force the kiss upon her, he brought all his sensual skill to bear and *persuaded* her to accept it.

Oh, this rat wasn't content to threaten her job or break her heart. He had to knock her self-esteem into smithereens. He rocked his mouth across her lips in exactly the way she had fantasized all through her teen years. Confident, hungry, enticing. Like he *loved* her.

Exactly as he'd just said he did.

She couldn't let his declaration affect her. It was a lie. She wanted to scratch his eyes out for playing with her like this.

Her own eyes stung, as if they'd been scraped raw behind her eyelids, but her self-control checked out. The besotted girl who had fallen in love so long ago came running out of her room, where she'd been crying into a pillow for five years. She threw herself into Isidora's body, heart singing with joy. She offered her mouth and drank up the sweet sensations that washed over her as Ramon acted, finally, like he wanted her.

Everywhere they touched, her skin bloomed with heat. Her bones turned pliant and the betrayal of his putting her on the spot like this evaporated. *Her*, the girl who had crushed so hard on a boy who was too old for her, the girl who had been ignored, rejected, then brutally passed over for her mother, the girl who had dealt with those horrible feelings of treachery and rebuff… She kissed him back.

She wasn't terribly experienced and that was his fault, too. These were the arms she had wanted from the first. These were the lips. This was the man.

He drew back and she realized he had one possessive hand drawing slow circles on her butt. That's why flutters of excitement were working up her lower back and into her loins. The fireworks that had been going off behind her closed eyelids were actually flashes. The roar in her ears was excited laughter and cheering. Sly jeering.

At her expense.

Oh, this mean bastard of a man. He didn't even let her go when she pressed her weak arms against his chest and tried to make space to catch her breath.

His embrace tightened to keep her smeared across his front. All she could do was hide her face by resting her ear against his chest and look toward the back wall—where Etienne stared at her with his lip curled in contempt.

"You—" So many filthy names crowded her tongue as Ramon closed them into his office minutes later that she couldn't pick one. "How *could* you?"

Her chest was tight, her voice fractured. Her entire world was topsy-turvy and it didn't help that she was in the mirror image of Henri's office, situated on the other side of a pair of connecting doors to her right. She definitely felt as though she stood on the wrong side of a looking glass.

Ramon threw off his jacket and slung it over the back of the sofa as he passed the conversation lounge. He dug his ringing phone from the pocket of his pants on his way to his desk in front of the tall windows.

"I need to take this. Stay here until you can find a suitable glow of delight. You looked like hell as we left. Good thing they only saw the back of you. *Hola.*"

"Are you serious?" a woman's voice said. It sounded like Trella, but she and Angelique sounded very similar.

Ramon propped the phone against his laptop dock and glared at it. "This is your fault. Say 'thank you.'"

Definitely Trella.

"Why would you do something like that to poor Isidora? She didn't know it was coming, did she?"

"Did I take you by surprise, *mi amor*?" He turned his head to glance at where she stood like a whipped dog, hovering inside the closed door, trying to find her bearings among the cool masculine colors and implacable lines of the décor.

"Izzy's with you? I'm so sorry, Izzy." Trella was one of the few people who could get away with calling her that.

"It's fine," Isidora lied, forcing herself to move until she was close enough to see both Trella and Angelique in the screen, but not so close she joined Ramon in the tiny window. "I should have found a way to defuse those photos before they became more than we could contain. But we'll need a statement from you. There's no more avoiding it."

"It's not your fault." Trella spoke in the same pained tone she had used each time Isidora had tried coaxing her toward a disclosure. "I know I have to cop to eating for two, but I don't want…"

To tell the father. That was obvious, since she refused to name him even to her family. They all had a very good idea, however. Isidora had concluded herself that the man in question had to be Prince Xavier of Elazar, who had been photographed kissing "Angelique" earlier this year.

As Ramon had said himself, Isidora had never had a

problem telling the twins apart. She had known straight away that *Trella* had been caught kissing that particular prince, while Angelique was the twin in the photos with Kasim.

Did Prince Xavier know which twin he had kissed? That was a question for another day. She imagined Angelique's fiancé, now *King* Kasim, must have some opinions on the matter as well, since his intended appeared to have two-timed him. But Angelique had never said a word on the topic. Today, she showed nothing but loving protectiveness as she looped an arm around her sister and gave Trella a comforting hug.

"Why don't I walk over right now and we can discuss some angles," Isidora suggested. She could use an excuse to leave the building and get some air.

"Pahahaha!" Trella sputtered.

"You can't!" Angelique cried at the same time, urgently shaking her head.

"Why not? Is there something going on at the design house—?"

"You're one of us now, *moza amiga.*" Trella leaned forward as though speaking to a child. "You travel by armored tank and avoid leading the hunters to the door. Seriously, *hermano.* What were you *thinking*?"

"What do you mean?" Isidora asked, even as reality began to sink in. Declaring a fake engagement, putting her on the spot in front of the cameras like that, had been awful, but the greater ramifications began to strike her consciousness.

No. The explosion of excitement downstairs had been for Ramon. Hadn't it? The paparazzi wouldn't think they had found a fresh target in *her*, would they?

She had never thought of herself as naive, but suddenly saw herself as the world's most gullible idiot.

"Have you talked to your parents?" Angelique asked with concern, voicing what was finally hitting Isidora's sluggish brain. "They're probably getting calls."

Her mother.

Isidora touched her brow. All those years she had spent lying to the world, including *to her own father*, spinning and downplaying her mother's affairs so their family wouldn't be talked about and vilified. Now every single tryst would be dug up. Her mother's past lovers might even throw their names into the ring of fame, just to have their moment in the spotlight. It didn't matter that her parents had eventually divorced over Francisca Villanueva's infidelity. She had cheated on Bernardo Garcia dozens of times and he would be forced to relive all of it. He would be humiliated all over again.

Isidora flung around to face Ramon. Of all the things he'd done, this was, by far, the worst. "I will never forgive you for this."

CHAPTER THREE

Isidora's mother answered her call with "Oh, *mi cielo*. Henri just called. Such thrilling news! You've always loved Ramon so much—"

"Henri called you?" Isidora interrupted, praying her mother's voice hadn't carried.

Ramon was focused on his own phone as it buzzed with incoming texts. *"Si,"* Ramon said to Isidora. "Henri was watching the press conference. He's sending a car for your mother now."

"Henri is worried reporters will descend on you," Isidora informed her mother.

Francisca would definitely say the wrong thing if she knew the engagement was a publicity stunt. Isidora didn't clear up her mother's misconception, and just said, "You should pack, Mama. Don't keep them waiting."

"Where is Ramon? I want to give him my love." It was a twist of the knife her mother had plunged into her heart five years ago.

Isidora didn't waste hatred on her own flesh and blood, though. She didn't even bother speculating why her mother had taken Ramon to her bed when she had known how her daughter felt about him. She had processed long ago that her mother had an illness. An addiction. It looked like a dependence on sex, but it was actually a broken, empty soul starving for love and admiration. She was permanently an abandoned adolescent, like a broken runaway, with the same lack of judgment and gaping emotional needs.

Isidora would never feed in to that heartache by rejecting or reviling her. She did what she could to protect her. That's why she held Ramon in such contempt. How could he take advantage of someone so vulnerable?

"Henri has spoken to both your parents. He's bringing them to Sus Brazos for a few days while things blow over," Ramon told her.

Don't put them together, Isidora wanted to protest. Her parents were weak-willed where the other was concerned. It always ended the same, with her mother cheating and leaving for another man while her father nursed a freshly shattered heart. The hairline fracture left in Isidora's heart pulsed with an old ache as she contemplated another round of emotional turmoil.

"Is that the doorbell, Mama?" Isidora broke in to her mother's breathy ramblings. "Tell the staff to ask for identification. Call me when you're settled. *Te amo.*"

Isidora ended the call and sent a text to her mother's housekeeper with the same instruction about checking for identity.

"So," Ramon said as their flurry of communication ended and they set aside their phones.

"Why?" she cried. "Why would you *do* that?"

Why had he said he *loved* her? It made it all the more hurtful. Thorny vines were tangled around her insides, squeezing and prickling. Half of it was self-recrimination. She would love to say she had gone along with it because she was a professional willing to sacrifice herself on the altar of her career. In truth, she had been so stunned, so *appalled* that he would exploit her old feelings in such a careless manner, she had been struck dumb.

"You know why. The retirement announcement wasn't working."

"Why *me*?" It was cruel. Her cheeks and throat and chest still burned, but when had he ever cared about hurting *her*?

"Was I supposed to come out as gay and propose to Etienne?" So blithe, shrugging off the damage he'd done. "I admit, that might have created a more effective stir, but maintaining *that* ruse for any length of time…?"

"Do you honestly think anyone is going to believe we're a couple?" She wanted to *kill* him.

"That's up to you, isn't it? I'm serious about you working on looking more pleased about marrying a Sauve-terre. We have an image to maintain," he added with a disdainful tilt of his lips.

"Quit making jokes! This isn't funny." Her pulse raced like she was being chased through a dark forest by a pack of wolves. "I am *not* marrying you."

"No," he agreed, the single word dropping her old hopes like china on concrete. "But you will play the part of my fiancée until the attention on our family dies down."

"Oh, right. When has that ever happened? No, Ramon. I refuse. Go ahead and fire me for insubordination. *Make my day.*"

He folded his arms and leaned his hips on the desk, his expression bored. "Are you done?"

"Are you implying I'm overreacting?" She was trembling, hands fisted at the ends of her tensed arms, entire body twitching with fight or flight. *"You're ruining my life."*

"Please," he scoffed. "This is your job. You're in front

of the cameras all the time, standing next to one of us, making statements that say nothing. It's more of the same."

"It's *not*. I'm fine as a Sauveterre minion, but I don't want to be the main event!"

"You're not a minion." He drew back a little, sending her an annoyed frown. "You're part of the inner circle. You know that."

"Since *when*?" His siblings might treat her that way, but *he* certainly didn't.

"I wouldn't have gone down today's route with anyone else, even if there had been other choices. We trust you. This is obvious by the position you hold. How is this news to you?"

"*You* trust me?" She refused to let herself believe it. Wouldn't allow it to be important. "After what you said this morning about making my life difficult? Or was it miserable? Either way, you're ticking all the boxes, aren't you?"

He didn't move, but his expression hardened. "Let's talk about how I really ruined your life, shall we? Clearly we have to get that out of the way before you'll be able to act like a grown-up."

No. She felt her throat flex as it closed around a cry of pain, like an arrow speared into her windpipe. Without a word, she spun and headed for the door.

A *snick* sounded as she approached it. Oh, he had not just locked it. She gave the latch a furious wriggle and yanked on the door, but nothing happened. It was oddly frightening. She didn't fear him exactly, but she was terrified of the feelings he provoked in her. They were always off the scale. And to lock her in and insist she talk about *that*?

No. Clammy sweat broke out on her forehead. Her hands and feet went icy cold.

She spun to see him behind his desk. His hand came away from a panel that he casually closed so the surface of his desk was smooth and unbroken once again.

"Why are you such a horrible person?"

"You know why. That is what I've been saying." He spoke in a flat, implacable tone. The fact that he didn't deny being reprehensible did nothing to reassure her. He moved to the wet bar near the sitting area and pulled out a bottle of anise. "Your preferred spirit, I believe?"

She didn't answer, thinking it strange that he would know that. It was a common drink in Spain, though. It was probably a lucky guess. He poured them each a glass.

"You know our family history, Isidora. You played with my sisters when they had forgotten how. You visited Trella when she imprisoned herself in Sus Brazos. You showed a preference for me when every other girl on the planet couldn't tell me apart from my brother and didn't bother to try. Come. Sit."

She stayed stubbornly by the locked door, arms folded, face on fire. She stood there and hated him for knowing how infatuated she had been. For talking about it like it was some cute, childish memory. Nostalgia for a first pet.

Most of all, she hated him for making her stand here and relive the morning when two of her most painful experiences collided and became an utterly unbearable one.

He leaned to set her drink on a side table and sipped his own, remaining standing, flinty gaze fixed on her resentful expression.

"I was flattered, but I couldn't take you seriously. You were too young."

She had known that. Eight years was a big gap and aside from a handful of boyish pursuits, he and his brother had always been beyond their years. Their sister's kidnapping when they were fifteen had very quickly matured them, then their father's early death had forced them to take control of an international investment corporation at twenty-one. They had been carrying tremendous responsibility for a decade. In many ways, Ramon was still too old for her.

"I don't care that you never wanted to date me." Lie. She cared. His disinterest had been demoralizing. "What I can't forgive is that you slept with my mother."

"I didn't sleep with her," he growled.

She snorted and looked away, working to keep her face noncommittal while she was dying inside, aching to believe that, but she wasn't stupid. The fact he would lie to her face about it made it even worse.

"Did you ask her?" he prompted.

"No!" As if she wanted details about any of the men her mother slept with, most especially *him*. "I didn't have to, did I? The evidence spoke for itself."

"The evidence," he repeated, tone light yet dangerous, increasing her tension.

"You were half-dressed, wearing a night's stubble, and the hood of your car was cold. It doesn't take a forensic scientist to figure out where you spent the night."

"I've never denied spending the night."

"In her bed. Two pillows were used. I *looked."*

"I reclined *on* her bed while she changed and removed her makeup. We were talking. Nothing happened. We went back downstairs and drank enough that I decided to sleep it off on the sofa. I woke when I heard you come in. I tried to tell you this at your father's birthday. You walked away."

"Oh, please. Once she realized I'd come home, she didn't say, 'Oh, by the way, Ramon spent the night, but it was completely innocent.' She asked how long I'd been there and looked guilty as hell."

"That—" He pointed at her. "That is the real evidence, isn't it? You don't think your mother can't bring a man home without making love with him."

True, but that was such a complex issue for her, she refused to go there.

"You've hit a hard limit, Ramon. The way my mother lives is not up for discussion. I *will* walk. And that's not why I think you're the scum of the earth."

His head went back as though the cold iron in her tone caught his attention. After a brief pause, he said, "If you're thinking *I'm* the one who can't spend a night with a woman and not have sex, you're wrong."

He was talking about Trella, she supposed. Her friend's struggle with anxiety was something that turned Isidora inside out every single time she thought about it, but she refused to let herself soften with empathy. To give him the benefit of the doubt.

"You want me to believe that's what you were doing that night?" She burned afresh with outrage and scorn. "Letting my mother cry on your shoulder? Then why didn't you say so when we met in the lounge? I asked you what you were doing there and you said she had been looking for company so you came home with her. You knew what I took from that. You knew *exactly* what I was thinking. If you didn't have sex with her, why did you let me believe you did?"

"Because you were eighteen and still carrying a torch." His voice was a sledgehammer. "It had to stop."

This moment was every bit as hard a hit as that moment had been, completely destroying any shred of hope she might have clung to. For a few seconds, she couldn't breathe. The agony was that all-encompassing.

She wasn't *still* carrying a torch, was she? She would swear she hadn't been.

Until he had kissed her. Something tentative had begun playing in the back of her mind in the last hour, though. She was waiting for time alone to relive that kiss and properly savor it. To build it into something it would never become.

How pathetic.

He was right. This childish yearning had to stop.

As the silence lengthened, something tickled her cheek. She wiped at it, discovering it was a tear.

He released a heavy sigh, which scored, speaking as it did of his impatience with her intense feelings where he was concerned.

She was equally exhausted by it herself. She really was.

Last one, she vowed. That was the last tear she would ever cry over this man.

Because it didn't matter if he had slept with her mother or not. What he was telling her, then and now, was that he would never be interested in her. Not as anything but a fake fiancée. A prop for one of his PR tricks.

She *had* to move on.

She nodded with understanding, feeling disconnected from her body. The muscles around her mouth twitched and she thought she might be trying to smile, but it was the kind that came when the tragedy was too great for any other emotion but laughter at how punishing life could be.

"Tough love," she said, voice jagged beneath the irony.

He swore and she heard him exchange his empty glass for the one she hadn't touched. He knocked back that shot and his breath hissed again.

"It was a test. You passed."

"Because I didn't turn on you and your family?"

Such a cold bastard. What had she ever seen in him?

Aside from his incredible devotion to his family, of course. And his unbending will to win, his lust-worthy looks, his charisma, brilliant intelligence and unwavering confidence.

She wanted to turn on him now.

But she couldn't. It wasn't in her to walk away from people who needed her. Even when her own heart was twisted beyond recognition by staying.

That was her specialty, in fact. Wasn't it? Helping her father and mother navigate the pain they caused each other, standing by both of them while they went through it. She carried on, fractured and battered by a heartrending personal life. Why should her professional life be any different?

Forcing herself to move, she closed herself into the powder room and checked her makeup. There was an emotive redness around her eyes and her lipstick was faintly smudged. She smoothed her hair and used a damp tissue to repair her lips, all the while thinking of the times her father had said he was proud of her. Not just for following in his footsteps, but for other things, too.

That love of his had pulled her through a lot—the devastation of learning he wasn't biologically her father, for instance.

Bernardo was her anchor, her moral compass, her silver lining in a world too often clouded and stormy. He was the parent her mother was incapable of being.

He would never wind up in such a ridiculous position, but if he had to choose whether to work with a Sauveterre or against one, she knew what he would do: whatever was asked.

He would stay loyal to the offspring of the man who had convinced him to accept the child her mother had passed off as his own.

Isidora owed the Sauveterres for the man she called "Papa," not that they knew it.

At least, when this was over, she would feel she had settled that debt.

Ramon savored the subtle bite of the anise, letting the fragrant sweetness roll on his tongue, thinking it was not unlike Isidora's personal flavor. *That kiss.* As he finally had a moment alone, he gave in to the memory of driving his tongue into welcoming heat. He had half expected her to drive her knee into his groin, but the kick of her response had been even more devastating. That hadn't been mere surrender. It had been a chemical explosion that had burned away everything he understood about kisses and women and sex.

What the hell?

He had held many beautiful women. None had sparked such a profound reaction in him. He had lost himself for a moment, absorbed in a vast landscape he instinctively knew would take a lifetime to explore.

Then the insanity of their public location had struck. He'd pulled out of the worst tailspin of his life, dazed and, yes, instantly defensive at having his thick shields penetrated so effortlessly.

If he had realized they were so sexually compatible—

No. He poured a third drink, refusing to go back and reexamine the turns he had already made. That was his brother's MO. Henri liked to track results on spreadsheets and weigh options as he made projections and charted his next moves. That invariably resulted in accurate predictions that efficiently achieved the result he wanted, but it wasn't Ramon's style. He let his gut pick the goal and shot toward it via the swiftest, shortest line, making corrections as problems cropped up.

His aim was to protect his family, first and foremost. Always. He never let his libido distract him. It was a weakness. Strength was his only option. Too many people depended on him, especially now that Henri had a wife and two defenseless infants to look out for.

But Ramon did have weaknesses. Some of them came around annually as a long, dark night of the soul. When he was not in a position to spend those nights with family, he sought company, usually female. That was how he had come to enter a bar in Madrid and find the ex-wife of his father's best friend, five years ago.

Francisca Villanueva was a delicate soul who carried a lot of pain. He had taken her home to keep less honorable men from taking advantage of her. He couldn't save her from herself indefinitely, but he could for a night.

She had made him laugh and revealed her own pain, exposing more cracks in her family than he had ever guessed from Bernardo's composed demeanor or Isidora's sunny smiles.

Coming face-to-face with Isidora as he left the next morning had been like one of those moments on a racetrack, where a split-second decision had to be made.

Isidora had been making calf eyes at him since adolescence. The longer her legs grew, the more difficult it was to ignore her. Temptation had been closing its grip on him as she blossomed into an ever more alluring woman, but she was too young and inexperienced for the light, temporary affairs he offered.

As her smile of delighted recognition had faded into confusion and suspicion, then betrayal and devastation, he had let the disillusionment happen.

He could have corrected her assumption. He could have told her that his night with her mother had been wine and conversation and a chaste kiss on the cheek when her mother went to bed alone. He could have kept Isidora's fixation on him alive, but to what end? He was never going to marry her. It wasn't personal. He would never marry anyone. Children were completely off the table. His siblings might be changing their minds about opening themselves to liability, but Ramon hadn't and wouldn't.

So what had been his alternative in that moment? Encourage Isidora to keep mooning after him? Eventually date her, sleep with her, *then* break her heart? No. He had used the opportunity to cut her off the lane she was on. Cruel, yes, but a type of kindness. She was on track to crash and burn otherwise.

He had not foreseen that Henri would hire her years later, but he couldn't argue with the appointment. Isidora had grown into a composed, accomplished woman with cutting-edge PR skills, and who possessed wit and intelligence. Most of all, she brought to the table a deep understanding of their family dynamics, allowing them to skip past painful history lessons.

Ramon accepted that she was angry. Hurt even. That she didn't want to lie about their being engaged. His proposal had been another reflexive move. Cruelty without kindness, but there was no backing out. They would have to make the best of it.

He stroked his thumb on the curve of the glass he held, trying not to fall back into dwelling on how exquisite her response had been. It was a dangerous distraction when he needed to stay focused on what his family needed.

The powder-room door opened and Isidora came out wearing an expression that was both calm and— Was that a light of joy as she let a broad smile take over her face?

It kicked him in the chest. *Dios*, there really was no ignoring how lovely she was.

"Better?"

His ears rang so loudly it took him a moment to catch the sarcasm.

"You said I could leave when I managed to look happy about this. Good enough?" She dropped her smile.

The radiance in her expression dimmed so fast and sharp, he felt it like the chill when the sun went suddenly behind a cloud.

"You'll need a retirement party and an engagement party," she continued matter-of-factly. "Two different ones, to maximize the coverage." She crossed to where she had left her phone. "We should do something around all the restructuring and promotions, too. We'll call them team-building sessions, but something visual, like zip lines or a fun run. We'll link it to a charity for a higher profile. You and I can make appearances, invite the press to watch you shake hands with your new CEOs. If I'm going to all this trouble to snag news coverage, Sauveterre International should benefit. I'll need a ring. Something flashy. Gaudy, even. The gossip outlets are on ring watch with Angelique so let's give them something to notice. I won't keep it, so I'll arrange a loan—"

"I'll get the ring," he interjected, not quite trusting this abrupt switch in attitude. "You're doing this, then? No more arguing?"

"Oh, I'm sure we'll argue, but you haven't given me much choice, have you?" She took a moment to set her shoulders and lift her chin, as though bravely facing down a firing squad.

Was it really such a monumental favor? He hitched his hands on his hips, wanting to roll his eyes. "You'll be compensated."

"That's not what I'm after." She flashed him a cross look, offended. "I'll always do what I can to help Trella.

All of your family. But… How long does this have to last? Three or four months?" Her brow furrowed with calculation. "Once Trella has her baby and Angelique announces her engagement, you and I can have a nice public breakup, yes? Unless something else comes up along the way and we need a story?"

Ramon knew when to push an advantage and when to simply hold on to one, but it still bothered him as he said, "That sounds appropriate."

"It will make sense that I leave the company when we part ways. You should talk with Henri about how you plan to replace me."

A reflexive protest rose, but she was right. He would facilitate her finding a good position as part of her compensation. After a suitable period, if they needed her, they could pull her back.

She cut him a glance and briefly bit her lip. The self-conscious color in her face increased. "Etienne would seem the natural choice for my position. If that's what you're thinking, I should disclose something."

He narrowed his eyes, not wanting to believe what had just leaped into his brain. "Continue."

She tucked a wisp of hair behind her ear, cleared her throat and smiled flatly. "He expected the promotion into my father's position. He's been upset about my receiving it."

"So? We make our decisions based on what's best for us."

"I know, but…" She clicked off her phone. "He worked under my father for the four years I was at school. I've never advertised how close I am with your sisters so he doesn't realize why you chose me. He feels passed over—"

"I don't care about his dented ego, Isidora. Why would I?"

"I'm telling you why." She dropped her phone into the pocket of her jacket and smoothed a fingertip along her eyebrow. "If you think he'll be appropriate to take my job, we should bring him in on this. Tell him the engagement is fake so he feels part of the team. He already thinks I earned my way on my father's coattails, but he and I used to date and—"

"You *slept* with that idiot." For some reason, Ramon had believed she was still a virgin. He knew it was outlandish, but she projected such innocence at times.

She lowered her lashes now, blushing like a new bride.

Of course a woman her age would have had lovers. He didn't know why it was such a surprise. Maybe because his sisters had never breathed a word about her dating exploits. Her father had spent Isidora's adolescence closely monitoring her virtue—which was absolutely no surprise given her mother's behavior. That vigilance of her father had been yet another reason Ramon hadn't so much as glanced in her direction, but he had honestly believed her attention had never strayed from *him*.

Despite the pains he'd taken to ensure it would.

So why did it bother him to discover she had followed her urges to other men? Maybe because he couldn't help wondering if she'd kissed them the way she had kissed him today. Had Etienne enjoyed fully the passion Ramon had only tasted?

Dios. It was one thing to know she had men in her past, quite another to pass the lothario in the hallway. To wonder if she carried a torch for *that* man.

"Etienne is not an idiot," she said stiffly. "He's dedicated and smart, otherwise my father wouldn't have apprenticed him and I wouldn't have kept him on. The important piece here is that he could become a liability if not handled carefully."

Ramon choked out a laugh, astonished by how much aggression filled him—he made his voice as callous and dispassionate as he possibly could.

"You're adorable. How have I treated you, Isidora? And you have value to me. You think I'm going to put on kid gloves for a spineless twit nursing entitlement issues? What did I say to him before the press conference? As far as the world is concerned, you just became part of my family. If he treats you with anything less than the utmost respect, if he makes one wrong step for any reason, he will lose his job." It was the same lack of mercy he showed anyone, but the clench in his chest pushed the words out with added vehemence. "More, if I judge him to be any sort of threat beyond rumor-mongering."

Her lashes went down and her cheeks went hollow.

"Do not even think of telling him that. If he needs it spelled out, his job is already lost." He couldn't countenance her wanting to protect the man. Did she still have feelings for him? "Only my siblings will know our engagement isn't real," he stated, halfway to firing Etienne for no other reason than that he existed. "Otherwise we'll be dismissed in a day and the press will go straight back to crucifying Trella."

"Fine," she said in a small voice. "But I have to tell my father it's fake."

"No."

"Yes, Ramon." Her lashes swept up, but rather than vehemence, he read a surprising vulnerability. Her voice held a tiny fracture. "He'll assume it's a stunt, same as your family did, but he'll expect me to confirm it. The alternative is for you to ask for my hand like a proper suitor and I won't let you lie to him. Not about that. It was bad enough you—" Color bled across her cheekbones and she clammed up, jaw tightening.

Said he loved her?

Something seesawed in his chest, but he had to agree. There was too much history with Bernardo. He'd been a true friend to their father and later a very trusted advisor to him and Henri. He couldn't disrespect Bernardo with any sort of lie.

"I'll speak to him," he promised.

"Thank you," she said stiffly.

"Good. Now let's get to work." His thoughts expanded as everything he had come to Paris to implement was now filtered through a fake engagement. He moved to his desk and opened the panel to release the doors, then asked his PA to assemble key personnel in the boardroom.

Isidora lingered.

"I thought you were anxious to escape? Call Julie," he told her. "She coordinates my calendar with my race schedule. Ask her to plan the retirement party in Monaco. Then join us in the meeting."

"Yes, fine," she said, brushing a hand through the air. "But I just want to be clear. No more passes like today." Her cheeks went bright pink.

"It wasn't a pass. It was a performance. More will be necessary."

Her jaw tightened. "Keep it to a minimum. I won't sleep with you."

It struck him that he had tied himself to the one woman he shouldn't sleep with, even if she wanted to—which he had taken great pains to ensure she didn't. *Dios!* Celibate? Him? He had to bite back a curse of self-disgust, but as he thought again about how open he'd left himself when he'd had her in his arms, he knew it was better to keep a lid on things.

"You weren't invited to," he stated.

Her stunned expression went stoplight-red, flashing blunt injury before she spun and treated him to a view of her rigid spine and spectacular ass. The door slammed loudly behind her.

CHAPTER FOUR

Isidora pasted on a smile as fake as her engagement and allowed Ramon the Rat to take possession of her life.

She knew how the Sauveterre men worked. There was no option to lead, only to follow or get out of the way. She had agreed to follow. As she sat through the meeting, she felt herself sucked along the slipstream of his accelerated pace. He snapped his whip over the team, pacing behind her and pausing only to consult with her in an offhand way as he threw out dates and locations, names and promotions.

"You agree, *mi amor*?"

"Of course, *cariño*," she murmured, smiling and smiling her manufactured joy until her face ached. Trying to hide that she was dying inside.

She didn't know how she would get through this.

The news that he hadn't slept with her mother altered her feelings drastically. Of course she was relieved, but the resentment that had been a form of protection had been burned to the ground, leaving her suddenly susceptible to the powerful attraction that had always gripped her.

Which had made his shot about not inviting her to sleep with him quite the poison dart. Her insides were still seared raw. What was it about this man that made her so ultrasensitive to him? Was she missing a vital gene of self-preservation? She really was her father's daughter, if that was the case.

Ramon had gone to incredible lengths to rebuff her and still didn't want anything to do with her. That indifference of his had done a number on her self-esteem in her teen years, but after a lot of travel and hard work at school, not to mention dating men who actually seemed to *like* her, she had built up her confidence. Maybe she hadn't fully escaped her fascination with Ramon, since she had never been drawn enough to other men to sleep with them, but she knew they found her attractive. Not that she needed a man to validate her. Her work ethic was solid and the work she did well-received. She had started today feeling like the confident, professional woman she had fought to become.

But she was back to feeling like an adolescent with an inferiority complex.

No. She had a thick skin in every other area of her life. Control, composure and staying on message, were her stock in trade. He had said this was just an extension of her job. She had to be as unaffected as he was.

As the meeting broke up, he chivalrously helped her with her chair.

She exerted supreme effort and kept her inner turmoil from her face, feeling brittle as she said, "Good meeting." She made to step past him.

His heavy hand landed on her hip, urging her to stay and face him. Her stomach trembled in reaction. The intimate tone of his voice picked at her composure, threatening to unravel it.

"We should celebrate."

It's for show, she reminded herself, holding very still, trying to ignore the gaping canyon of yearning that opened inside her. His light touch sent licks of fire up her side and down her thigh. She told herself it was okay if her cheeks revealed the heat radiating from her core, that she was supposed to be dazzled by him. She gave in to his power for one moment and let her adulation of this particular god shine through her expression.

A startled spark flashed in his gaze, exciting and terrifying at once. His other hand came to her other hip and his fingers tightened. His attention slid to her mouth.

Her lips tingled as though he'd grazed them with his own. The memory of their kiss was right there, making her heart begin a rapid drumbeat.

You weren't invited to.

She had folded like a cheap tent for him the first time, but a jagged catch of humiliation kept her from doing it again.

She didn't care if they had an audience to amuse. The people filing toward the door were sending them curious smirks, but sick horror took hold in her, tensing her with resistance. She would not allow herself to become a laughingstock.

"Let's keep the PDA to a minimum in the office, *hermoso*. No need to embarrass anyone." She set her hand firmly on his chest, face averted. "I'll go make a reservation for dinner."

His strength was such that he didn't have to exert himself one iota to keep her exactly where she was. "I'll arrange it."

"You mean you'll ask Monique to do it?" She batted her lashes as she mentioned his PA. Engagement banter. So cute.

"I said *I* would." His voice was laconic, his expression arrogant. Yet watchful enough to make the moment feel bizarrely lethal.

She was in the cage with the tiger. His tail was twitch-

ing, but he wasn't hungry. Not for her. She was safe.
For now.

"Seven o'clock?" he asked.

"Can't wait." She tried again to pull away and this
time he allowed it.

And she knew she was deranged on some level because disappointment clawed in her chest.

Isidora did her own makeup and hair, then put on a dress
her mother had bought for her when they were shopping
on her last birthday. She had only tried it on because her
mother had insisted.

"You have such a beautiful figure, *mi angel*. Why
don't you show it off?"

Isidora had bit back observing that her mother did
enough showing off for both of them. "It's not exactly
office attire, Mama."

It was a strapless cocktail dress that hugged her curves
in what looked like ribbons of liquid gold. The tails came
together in a bow between her breasts, leaving a peeka-
boo cut out over her diaphragm.

"You work too hard. Dance!" Her mother had bought
her a pair of gold heels to go with it. "Enjoy your youth.
Live your life with *entusiasmo*!"

Francisca was an heiress who had grown up with everything except love and discipline. The expense of a
designer outfit for her daughter was nothing compared
to what her mother spent on herself each month. Isidora
had accepted the gift, fully expecting it would collect
dust in her closet.

She never wore skirts this short. Given her mother's
lack of modesty, she compensated with conservative
styles and even more conservative behavior. Ramon's
sisters could easily get away with showing this much

skin and still look respectable, but Isidora felt positively loose and looked…ah, hell. She looked like her mother. Not so much physically, but in the come-hither display of her wares.

She never dressed like this, especially for a man. Ramon's constant rejections during her adolescent years had killed that in her.

She might have panicked and changed, but as she took note of the text that Ramon was on his way, she noticed things were heating up online. Ugh. She checked the rest of her notifications with dismay. She would have to discuss that with him.

In danger of running late now, she closed the door of her flat and descended the two flights of stairs to the lobby, realizing as she arrived on the bottom step that the noise she had dimly assumed was a neighbor's television was actually a crowd gathered outside the glass doors of her building.

Aside from a handful of photographers, her arrival home from work hadn't drawn much notice, but in the hour she'd been dressing, a hundred people had gathered. Maybe more.

She instinctively hung back until a black car pulled up to the curb.

An excited murmur grew. Ramon's guard stepped from the passenger seat, took a reading on the crowd and directed people to part, waiting until there was a clear path to the building's door before he opened the rear door of the car.

Ramon rose with his easy grace. The crowd roared with approval.

He paused to give them a nod, utterly breathtaking in close-cut pants and a light blue pullover beneath a linen blazer. He really was too beautiful.

Isidora snapped out of her admiration and quickly moved through the lobby and out the doors, intent on keeping the spectacle to a minimum and allowing them to hurry away.

As she appeared, another roar went up.

She paused reflexively, not expecting the reaction. She was no one. Fake, fake, fake.

They didn't know that, of course. They went wild.

She found her party smile and waved a greeting.

Was this what it was like for them? Pretending to be happy about the attention? Pretending she enjoyed the claps and calls of her name?

Wait. Was that a curse? A *boo*?

She faltered, glancing to the right where someone said something she didn't catch, but his tone was aggressive.

The mood of the crowd shifted. The excited babble grew bothered as people jostled. She heard someone say something about her destroying the sport.

It was unnerving and she took a few more steps forward, but there were no ropes or other obstacles to hold people back. The crowd on either side had pressed into the space, narrowing her path, and a woman stumbled into her way, crying out a protest at being shoved. The milling bodies grew more unruly and an unseen hand reached for Isidora, hard fingertips skimming her arm.

Startled, she jerked from the touch, staggered in her heels and wound up bumping into someone on the other side.

Like walls closing in, strangers pushed into the space between her and Ramon, blocking her from both him and a safe retreat into her building as they started to surround her.

She grew scared. Truly scared. She looked for him,

but another touch on her arm had her jerking her head around.

She was given a hard yank and lost her footing. She stumbled toward the sidewalk, hands outstretched.

Ramon was unsurprised that a crowd had gathered outside Isidora's building. It was routine when he started dating a woman that fans and paparazzi tried to catch a photo of him with his new woman. It was the reason women threw themselves at him—for the notoriety.

He had expected to go into the building and escort Isidora out. That was also routine. He was a gentleman who offered door-to-door service, but she stepped out as he arrived, then paused in surprise as the crowd reacted.

He, too, reacted. His breath left him as he took in the vision she made of polished gold against the weathered stone of her building. She was an award statuette come to life, loose auburn curls gently shifting around her bare shoulders, her legs pale, delectable stems that begged for kisses upon every inch.

His gut tightened exactly as it had when he had stood in his boardroom, keeping her standing before him, feeling her hold him off even as she turned her sunny expression up to him.

He had basked in the glow of her smile like a cave dweller in springtime, startled by how good it felt. He had missed that light. That warmth. For a few seconds, an unidentified tightness in him had eased. He had wanted to kiss her again. Hard and deep. The kind of kiss that didn't stop until they were both replete.

He wanted to make love to her. He could lie to her and pretend he didn't, but he couldn't lie to himself. What man, looking at her now, would *not* want to carry her to the nearest bed? She was breathtaking.

Desire like he had never known crystalized in him, far more potent than the generic sexual hunger that pulsed in his loins for any woman who gave him a signal. His body suddenly demanded *this* woman. He needed *her* capitulation. *Her* writhing body beneath his.

Pure lust blinded him as surely as their kiss had—which became a near fatal mistake as the crowd turned on her.

It was not something he had ever experienced. Female fans might say jealous things about his dates online, but no woman he'd ever been with had ever been assaulted.

Nevertheless, in seconds, the avid excitement in the crowd became stained with hostility. Outright aggression. Isidora was shoved and started to fall.

He reacted with the reflexes he had honed on the track and hardened with physical training, which included military-style fighting. He shoved aside whomever stood between them, swept her up and growled, "Get back or I'll kill you."

Not his usual urbane reaction, but he was incensed. Shaken. Utterly feral in that moment, unnerving himself and terrifying pale faces into backing off with wide-eyed alarm.

Oscar, his day guard, was right there, arms spread to ensure the press of bodies gave them room to reach the car. Ramon slid Isidora into the back seat and threw himself in behind her, slamming the door to lock them in. His heart jammed and his temperature redlined.

"What the *hell*?" he groaned as Oscar leaped into the passenger side and the driver took off down the street, pressing them into their seats.

"I had no indication—" Oscar stammered.

"It's because you quit racing *for me*," Isidora said in a small, breathless voice. She was white as a sheet, looking back through the rear window at the uprising they had barely escaped.

"Qué?" He couldn't process that she had an answer when his security guard didn't.

"Some, um…" She cleared her throat, visibly trying to regain her composure as she faced forward and folded one trembling hand over the other. "Some of your fans think your proposal was romantic, but some are blaming me for their favorite driver leaving their favorite sport."

"You knew this was brewing and didn't warn me?" The top of his head nearly came off.

"I started seeing the posts a few minutes ago." Her face was drawn, her tone distraught. "I was going to tell you now. When I saw you."

"It's protocol to forward security concerns the second threats are recognized."

"When they target you or your siblings. They weren't saying anything against you, so I…" Her eyes nearly ate up her face at whatever was in his expression. Her voice became so thready, he barely heard her. "I didn't think—"

"No. You didn't. You put me in danger, Isidora. All of us." He waved at Oscar and his chauffeur, then pulled out his phone and connected to the man who held the contract for Sauveterre security.

"We need a full detail for Isidora. Everything my sisters have."

A preliminary backup team was immediately organized to join them at the restaurant. A promise was made to have everything in place by morning.

"I thought they were just trolls," Isidora muttered.

"And I thought Trella's kidnapper was just Gili's math tutor. *Anything* could have happened back there." He was still beside himself, his thoughts in the darkest places because he had learned the hard way that those places were real. "You could have been trampled. Beaten. Thrown into the street under a car. Stolen and raped and killed. *You should have warned me*."

What if that had happened? What if it had been his fault?

She pushed back into her seat, lips white, chin crinkled, eyes blinking hard. Her knees were pressed together tight, her painted fingernails clutching her elbows. With a little sniff, she turned her face away and her throat flexed.

"Scared? You damn well should be!"

She hated him *so much*. And she would not—*would not* let him make her cry.

"Whose fault is it that they hate me?" she choked out. *"Yours."*

"You think I don't know that?" he roared.

She jolted and even the driver was startled because the car juddered before he smoothly changed lanes and carried on.

With a curse, Ramon leaned forward and closed the privacy screen.

"*This* is why I'm such a bastard. *This* is why I don't compromise. *This* is why I can never be the man you wanted me to me." He sat back, fist hitting his thigh. His voice held a note of uncharacteristic defeat. "I could never ask a woman to put up with this for the rest of her life."

Your brother did, she wanted to snap out, but Henri and Cinnia had broken up and only came back together when Cinnia was noticeably pregnant. If she hadn't been carrying a Sauveterre, Isidora was pretty sure both brothers would have remained bachelors their entire lives.

She privately believed Henri had been glad to have the excuse to get back with Cinnia. He had sounded indescribably pleased when he had told Isidora they were married, but Ramon seemed resolved in his detachment.

And looked surprisingly lonely in it. He stared ahead, his profile a study in carved planes and stark shadows.

"I'm sorry," she said in a subdued tone.

"You should be."

Why did she even bother? She looked out her window again, shoulders aching where she refused to let them slouch, trying not to breathe so he wouldn't hear her sniff.

As he waited for Isidora outside the powder room on the top floor of the Makricosta Elite, Ramon was more keyed up than before a race.

He had set her up for harm with his proposal.

From the time he was fifteen, after Trella had been stolen and recovered, he had settled into a mostly unspoken agreement with his brother. Neither of them would pursue a serious, long-term relationship. A Sauveterre wife, and most especially a child, would be endangered simply by carrying their name.

Cinnia's accidental pregnancy had forced his brother to change his mindset, but Henri had had feelings for Cinnia from the beginning, whether he had admitted to them or not.

Ramon kept his heart far more guarded. The logistics of protecting the people he cared about was a big responsibility, but that wasn't the only reason he refused to marry. He had the money and resources to ensure the best if it came down to it. No, the real issue was the emotional cost. The idea that a woman he cared about, or a child he loved, could be taken and harmed as Trella had been, closed such a fist of terror in Ramon, he could barely withstand it.

He didn't like being that vulnerable. He was very judicious in how much he cared and for whom. It was why he strove for indifference in his sexual relationships.

His proposal to Isidora had been a stunt. It was supposed to look gallant. In the back of his mind, he'd been aware that extra security precautions would have to be taken. Any woman who was attached to him was entitled to his protection. His team knew the drill.

But this sort of attack? The preliminary report on the social-media diatribe had since come through and the vehemence against Isidora was unnerving. Ramon felt like an idiot—not something he was used to. He was furious with himself for not anticipating it. He knew how much evil existed in this world. How had he not guessed this could happen?

Fear for her pierced his thick shields and maintained a thorny hold on him. He did what he could to alleviate it by biting out terse orders at his guard. "Send a team to her apartment. She's not going back there. She'll stay with me."

Oscar nodded as he texted.

She emerged, pale with stark shadows in her eyes, and checked when she saw him. Whatever was in his grim expression made her sweep her lashes down to hide her thoughts before she lifted her chin.

"You didn't have to wait for me. I'm perfectly capable of finding my way to the table without getting egged."

It hadn't even occurred to him to go ahead. He thought of all the times Trella had asked him to wait outside a bathroom door, suffering panic attacks so debilitating she had been afraid to be alone for five minutes. For once it had been his own apprehension that had kept him standing sentry.

"Let's not test that."

She flinched at the rasp in his tone.

He grimaced, but only waved at her to precede him.

The maître d' greeted them warmly and showed them to their best table, where a bottle of Dom Pérignon stood chilled and ready. The table was set with bone china, gold cutlery and gold-rimmed champagne flutes. Rose petals adorned the white cloth. Three glittering candles stood sentinel over a delicate spray of white orchids with pink centers. The exotic blooms curled around a small velvet box in a fragrant embrace.

Which is when Ramon remembered placing a request for some pageantry this afternoon, after Isidora had looked so pithy about his making a reservation, like she knew damn well he didn't call restaurants himself.

He didn't, but he had a competitive streak a mile wide. It demanded he prove someone wrong even when they were right.

"I'll give you a moment." The maître d' retreated.

Isidora said nothing, just stood there staring, freshened lipstick seeming stark against her pale face.

In his periphery, he noted that people were openly watching.

"It was supposed to be a joke," he groaned beneath his breath.

"I know." Her voice was faint. She brought her hand up to steady her trembling mouth. The sheen on her eyes grew thicker.

She'd had a shock, he realized belatedly, and he'd been treating her like the altercation at her building was her fault. It wasn't. It was *his* fault, for being who he was. Nothing could change it, either. He had had come to grips with that years ago.

She, however, had been on the sidelines. Until today, she hadn't known how it really was, and that was only the tip of the iceberg.

He reached out on instinct, pulling her trembling body into his.

She stiffened, arms cool and hesitant as they tucked like bent wings into the space beneath his jacket, against his rib cage. He smoothed a hand down her tense back, startled by how slight she felt. This spine of hers was hammered steel. He'd seen it in the way she had shown it to him for five years.

The competitor in him loved the challenge this narrow back represented. As she had held him off after their meeting, disparaging what was a typical effortlessness when it came to seducing a woman, the idea of showing her he was perfectly capable of romance had seemed inordinately pleasing.

Then, everything had turned inside out.

This wasn't a game. He had endangered her with this engagement and they couldn't call it off because he wasn't going back to racing. For the next few months at the very least, she needed his protection.

All they could do was play the part and hope that the impression of true love turned the tide.

"Let's get this over with," he murmured, reaching for the velvet box.

Isidora made a choked sound, too disheartened to be a laugh.

For some reason, the sound hit like a missile, landing in a place he hadn't known was unguarded, making him uncharacteristically unsure as he revealed the oval-cut diamond. It reflected the peacock-blue topaz stones that flanked it. On first glance it was beautiful in its simplicity, but on closer inspection, the complexity of the cut and setting became a reward for a lengthier study. It was quietly radiant, much like its new owner.

Ramon said what had been in his mind when he chose

it. "It's not on loan. I want you to keep it. As a thank-you for doing this."

Isidora's expression revealed nothing. Her hand held a fine tremor as she allowed him to work the ring onto her finger, but that was her only reaction. Her face looked like it was made of porcelain.

He was unaccountably disappointed. He'd chosen this piece because he had genuinely thought she would like it. Most women grew quite exuberant when offered jewelry.

"You don't care for it?"

"It's beautiful." Her voice sounded constricted. To anyone overhearing them, she would have sounded as overcome as a newly engaged woman ought to. Her lashes flickered as she took in the extravagant display once more.

Finally, she looked at him. Her eyes were bruised mauve in the candlelight, filled with the disillusionment he'd seen the morning at her mother's.

"It's the proposal of my dreams."

Ah, hell.

He took in the image he'd projected with this setup, seeing how thoroughly he had played to every woman's fantasy, not thinking that this particular woman would have imagined this moment, with him, over and over, once upon a time.

"No other man could ever top it." Her smile was harder than the diamond she now wore. "Thank you."

It was supposed to be a joke.

His ribs felt like they'd curled to bite into his lungs.

She barely spoke through their entire dinner.

"Are you high? I am not moving in with you." Seriously, could this day get any worse? Ramon's driver had just missed the turn to her flat and Ramon had thought that was the right time to mention he wanted her to live with him for the duration of their engagement.

Like. Hell.

Dinner had devolved into a series of selfies with restaurant patrons unable to resist a snap with the infamous Sauveterre. Neither of them had protested the rudeness. It had saved them from speaking to each other.

In the privacy of his car, however, she had plenty to say. Pointing at the ring on her finger, she said, "Exactly how much cooperation do you think this buys?"

"As much as I require."

His face was impossible to read in the uneven flicker of light beyond the car, but the air seemed to crackle. Her ears pulsed with the suddenly hard beat of her heart. It seemed to fill the canned space they occupied, the back seat suddenly far too small for the two of them.

As the silence played out, a weird fear accosted her.

Let him say he thought he owned her. Let him reach across and act like he would prove it.

She wanted to believe this sting in her veins was readiness to scratch his eyes out if he tried, but deep down she knew what really scared her. That she might let him touch her. She might even like it.

"The fact my team was able to empty your flat, robbing you blind without one person trying to stop them, tells me how effective your security is." He was contemptuous, not contrite, and returned his attention to his phone.

Or maybe her deepest fear was that he would never touch her again.

A huge lump lodged in her throat. She fought back the sense of rawness, of fresh rejection, clinging instead to anger at his high-handedness.

"So I don't have anything to go home *to*? I have half

a mind to report you to the police." The zip of motor scooters flying up beside them, trying to get a snapshot of them through the darkened windows, dissuaded her.

But did he have any idea how badly he'd hurt her today? Mocking her most cherished dream, saying things like "let's get this over with"?

"Can't I go stay with your sisters at Maison—"

"It's a big space," he interrupted, biting off each word. "You won't see me if you don't want to."

It was. The six-bedroom penthouse belonged to his family and she took a room at the far end from his.

For the next week she passive-aggressively texted him, rather than walk down the hall to speak to him. She didn't eat breakfast with him, taking care to eat while he worked out.

She had to join him in the car to go to work, but she did her best to keep to her own office through the day. He was busy with the restructuring and she was busy planning their fake engagement junket. They worked late every night, which allowed him to cry off his many social invitations, thank goodness. They ate whatever dinner his housekeeper left for them, but she avoided him then, too. She worked out while he ate, then ate alone in the kitchen while he watched the news in the lounge.

She knew she was being childish, but every single minute in his presence was excruciating. When she had to act the part and set her hand on his arm or go up on tiptoe to peck his cheek, she felt worse than an open book. She was a story being read aloud, one that was gauche and predictable.

His scent would intrigue her nostrils, the feel of his stubbled cheek would brand her lips and she would have to fight the urge to draw out the contact. Her physical infatuation was as strong as ever and she was terrified he knew it.

Being alone with him was a million times worse. She was sensitive to his disapproval, and his ignoring her stung. She felt utterly defenseless. It was exhausting.

Now they had arrived in Monaco. Instead of being hands-off, ostensibly out of respect for office sensibilities, more overt displays of affection would be expected. They faced a string of parties and public appearances.

She didn't know how she would keep herself together, especially when she saw what close quarters they'd be in.

His pied-à-terre in the Carré d'Or of Monte Carlo was at the top of a former hotel. Its quirks of low ceilings and small rooms had been overcome with a clever layout and the opening of walls into grand archways, giving the space a wonderfully bright and airy feel. Its terraces overlooked the beach and sea, as well as the race circuit.

Under other circumstances, she would have been charmed beyond words, but it had only one bedroom. One *bed.*

"I'm not staying here," she stated when they were alone, the chauffeur having exited after dropping their luggage.

Ramon lowered the phone he was reading, the distracted lift of his head arrogant in the extreme. While she drowned in awareness every minute of every day, he barely noticed she was alive.

"Why do you say that?" he asked absently.

His power-soaked good looks were on full display in a collared shirt that clung to his shoulders and tailored pants that hung with sharp creases to his polished Italian shoes. He'd always been clean-shaven, but hadn't shaved today. The light stubble accentuated his masculinity. One glance from his gray-green eyes used to destroy her, and in one glance, she nearly succumbed all over again.

"Because there's only one bed." She hid her blush by glancing at the sofa, not keen on sleeping there, either. She had a good idea what had gone on here over the years. "This is where you bring your groupies after races, I presume?"

With one dismissive blink, he said, "I deliver."

Gross.

"Well, I don't," she stated firmly, and started to retrieve her luggage.

"It's one night." His tone hardened. "It's the most secure building in the city and my team knows the neighborhood. This is where we're staying. Use the sofa if you don't want to share the bed."

He went back to his phone like he didn't care if she camped in the bathtub.

He had a point about security. How did he live like this? She didn't want to soften toward him at all, but she was being handled by the kind of detail that followed him and his siblings and it was claustrophobic. She couldn't help feeling sorry for the bunch of them because she felt plenty sorry for herself.

She would prefer to be under protection than without it, though. The threats against her hadn't grown worse, but they were still awful. She knew the safest place she could be was at his side. In his secure flat.

She'd be safest of all in his bed, no doubt. He had never been interested in her and had shown more attention to his phone this week than to her. She was little more than someone's dog he was minding. *Here girl, sit. Stay.*

Blowing out a breath that made her fringe tickle her eyebrow, she threw her suitcase onto the bed and opened it, took out her makeup bag and locked herself in the bathroom.

She had squeezed in a fitting with his sisters the day after her "engagement" and they had put a rush on several items for her. Tonight she would wear a backless jumpsuit with a halter front in emerald-green. The vague nod to his racing overalls had seemed cheeky and fun when she'd chosen it for tonight's party, but as she pulled it on, insecurity struck.

It clung to her backside and thighs, coating her curves in shimmery green.

Ramon hadn't said anything about the gold dress she had worn to their engagement dinner. She had kept to her own outfits since, telling herself she didn't care what he thought of her, but tonight she would be judged against every supermodel who had ever dangled from his arm. She had to look her best.

She curled her hair, then shook the loose ringlets around her shoulders. The sparkle of her gold pendant drew attention to her cleavage. With the sinfully high shoes she had charged to Ramon on a passive-aggressive whim, all she could think was that she looked like she was trying too hard.

Insecurity struck as she relived all those times she had thought combing her hair a different way might be the ticket to finally catching his eye. Nothing she'd ever done, whether it was a new shade of lip gloss or a pricey push-up bra, had ever prompted the tiniest show of interest from him. She didn't want to be that girl again, obvious in her yearning and devastated when she fell short.

With a glance at her suitcase, which had nothing else to offer because they were only here one night, and a glance at the clock, she knew she was stuck. It wasn't as if she wore a minidress and bare legs, she told herself as she left the bedroom, heart in her throat.

At the sound of the door, Ramon stood and pushed his arms into a dark blue jacket over a pale gray shirt he wore open at the throat. He finished reading and dropped his phone, freezing as he glanced toward her. He took his time drifting his gaze from her carefully made up smoky eyes to her pedicured toes in rose pink.

The only noise came from the distant move of traffic far below the open terrace windows. As time inched along, her insides wobbled.

"Will I do?" she challenged, and did a slow pirouette, mostly so she could turn her back on him and gather her composure. She gave her hair another flip and felt his gaze strike her butt like a spank.

Get a grip, Isidora.

"Blame your sisters if you don't like what you see." She faced him again, and pretended her clutch needed a thorough inventory of its lipstick, mobile phone and credit card.

"I do like it," he said, voice hitting a low note that made her belly contract. He finished shrugging on his jacket. "You look beautiful."

"You don't have to be polite," she said flatly. "I mean, be polite, obviously, but don't say things because you think it's expected. I know I'm a scarecrow in your eyes. This extra effort is for the cameras, not you." She shook out a black chiffon jacket, startled when he was suddenly right beside her, taking it to hold it for her.

He smelled divine and looked sexy as anything with that five o'clock shadow and his dark brows pulled into a frown of admonishment. "I've always thought you were beautiful."

He sounded sincere, but it only made her sternum ache that he wasn't being honest with her.

"Seriously, save it for someone who wants to hear it."

He narrowed his eyes. "It's time to get over your anger, Isidora. Life's too short."

"I'm doing everything you ask," she snapped, taking back her jacket and tugging it on. "What else do you want from me?"

She flashed a look up, expecting the tired, remote look of boredom he seemed to have carved specially into his face for when he looked at her.

There was an eerie stillness in his stony expression, but the spark in his eyes turned them electric green. The air shimmered as though heated, spilling excitement, heady and thrilling, through her.

It was her turn to stall with one arm in a sleeve, grappling with an outlandish impression that she was not the only one fighting attraction. More like they were both fighting this *thing* between them, but the more they chipped at it, the closer they were to crumbling and crossing to the other side.

He was a formidable man. He had a special hold over her, but in that moment, she didn't feel small and helpless. She felt exalted. Empowered.

At the same time, attraction didn't merely tug at her. It drew her taut from the inside, threatening to swallow her whole.

He's doing it again.

With a muted gasp, she forced herself to pull back a step. Her heart thundered with panic, which she hid by finishing the yank of getting her jacket into place, nearly tearing the delicate fabric in her haste.

"Ask me that again when you're ready to hear the answer." His voice coiled around her, squeezing until she could hardly breathe, holding her in merciless thrall for one second as he lazily reached for the door.

He held it open, sending her an unreadable look as he waved an invitation for her to escape this airless apartment.

CHAPTER FIVE

RAMON'S RETIREMENT PARTY was held in the rooftop ball-room of a casino. A band played all the latest hits and a disco ball sent rainbow flecks bouncing off the mirrored columns that stood between draped alcoves. The guests, some of whom he considered friends, others merely faces he knew, were taking full advantage of the open bar, dancing in a crush on the floor and gambling enthusiastically where tables were set up in an adjoining room. It was a photo op and give-back to the racing community that had embraced him all these years. No expense had been spared.

Ramon liked parties. He was the extrovert of the family, but he couldn't seem to relax and enjoy this one.

"She's not what I expected," one of Ramon's toughest competitors, Kiergen Jensen said, as he gazed at Isidora dancing with Ramon's test driver. "Too nice for a man who stops at nothing to win."

Here, at least, Isidora wasn't being vilified for his departure from the track. She was lauded. His rivals were ecstatic they had a shot at the championship without him in the way and admired her for stealing the heart of such a confirmed bachelor.

Little did they know she hated him more than ever.

She had a right to be angry. He had put her in danger

and made a mockery of her childhood dreams. The job she had already struggled to prove wasn't pure nepotism had been turned into something even more blatantly biased. She had made it clear she wanted him to leave her alone, so he had.

But her enmity grated at him.

He had moved her into his space, something he had never done with a woman in his *life*. She resented it, and had gone back to leaving a room if he entered it. At work, she did a credible job of gushing if put on the spot, but she made sure everyone knew they intended to behave professionally. It was her way of avoiding physical contact. When he did have to act like a smitten suitor and take her arm or press a hand to her back, she stiffened. It was subtle, but he felt it. She didn't even want a compliment from him.

He was an egocentric man. He looked after himself, but had the capacity to love and worry for his family. He had even made accommodations in his life for his infant nieces. That's how he'd wound up at this retirement party. But he didn't reserve a lot of bandwidth for worrying about anyone outside his chosen few. Using Isidora for his publicity stunt had been expedient. Whatever cost she incurred as a result could be compensated monetarily. Her feelings had never been much of a factor in this.

So why did her antagonism bother him so much?

Then, as they were leaving to come here, it had become obvious. *Sexual tension*.

In the privacy of his apartment, with no one to see it, she had revealed—very briefly—that she was still attracted to him. Which was adorable, given their history.

He really wished he could dismiss the discovery that cavalierly, but he'd taken it like a bullet to the chest. He'd been aware of her all week. Hell, he'd always been *aware* of her. Now that she was grown and under his nose, it was impossible to ignore how alluring she was. She could wear subdued business attire and a sober office persona, hold herself beyond his reach and mutter pithy comments under her breath, but that had only fed his intrigue. Turns out, he had a depthless appetite for sexy-librarian fantasies and they all starred her.

Then, tonight, he had nearly popped a blood vessel when she had emerged looking chic and feminine in a skin-tight suit that revealed more than it disguised. She was utterly delectable and Kiergen wasn't the only one to notice.

The entire room, heavily weighted to high-octane men, found her mesmerizing. Why wouldn't they? She had her mother's ingenuous way of tilting up a wide-eyed gaze so all a man could think about was taking her under his wing. She also possessed her father's ability to draw people out. Her natural empathy made her anyone's immediate best friend. Add in her quick wit and unstoppable smile and she was irresistible.

She didn't lap up the attention the way another woman might, either, which only added to her attractiveness. He *felt* lucky to be with her, which was a singular sensation for a man who had always been the prize.

"I'd do whatever she asked of me, too." Kiergen's eyes stayed a little too long on Isidora's hips as she enjoyed herself on the dance floor.

"Hey." Ramon waited for his friend's gaze to track back to his, then shook his head. He meant it, and Kiergen knew it, which wasn't comfortable. Ramon hated being obvious. Revealing any detail about his wants or intentions, about what he valued, was something that could be used against him. He rarely exposed his throat.

He couldn't stop himself, though. With one question,

Isidora had released a roar of desire in him. *What else do you want from me?*

The list had been so long, he hadn't known where to start, but the way her tongue had absently dampened her lips had given him an idea.

He couldn't stop wondering what would have happened if she hadn't dragged her antipathy back into place along with her filmy wrap.

They wouldn't have made it to this party, that was for damn sure.

The song ended and she motioned that she needed a drink. She wound her way through the crowd toward him and Ramon handed across the glass that had been delivered while she'd been dancing.

"I had my chauffeur bring this up for you. For your father," Kiergen said, giving her a key fob that advertised his team logo.

Isidora had already fan-girled over Kiergen, claiming she and her father were both avid race followers, even though Ramon would have sworn she hadn't watched in years. Certainly not in person.

Her fawning over Kiergan had been annoying enough. Now Kiergen, the narcissist, was trying to keep the admiration train going with his penny candy swag.

Isidora's face brightened all the same. "I would have settled for a selfie, but thank you so much."

"We can do that, too." Kiergen's arm looped casually around her shoulders as she took the snap. He sent another smirk Ramon's way and hardened his arm to keep her close as she lowered her phone. "But now you have to answer something for me. I'm dying to know if you've ever kissed Henri."

Isidora pulled away in shock. "What?"

Ramon knew what was coming and his hackles rose even as Kiergen thumbed toward him.

"This one tried to kiss Cinnia. Did you never hear that story?" Kiergen grinned his enjoyment as Ramon glowered a warning. Isidora wouldn't see the funny side of it.

Kiergen couldn't resist, however, and launched into the tale that had become a small legend in their circle.

Shortly after Henri and Cinnia had become exclusive, Henri had brought her to watch one of Ramon's races. The next morning, as their usual group had gathered for breakfast, Henri had stepped away to take a call.

Ramon had been puzzled by his brother's fascination with her. Until Cinnia, neither of them had stuck with any particular woman more than a handful of days, let alone gone back for a particular one and locked her in for the foreseeable future.

Ramon had been high on his recent win and, well, sometimes brothers were jackasses to each other for the sake of it. Whatever had possessed him, he had mimicked Henri's preferred French greeting, moved behind where Cinnia sat, set his hand on her shoulder and leaned in to kiss her just as if he was Henri.

Maybe it had been a test. His brother was plenty sharp enough to look after himself, but there had been a part of Ramon that had needed to know how sincere Cinnia's feelings for Henri really were.

"We all thought he was Henri," Keirgen was saying. "For about one second she did, too. Then, right before he kissed her, she screamed. Jumped a meter. I thought she was going to punch him. Henri came running, ready to draw blood. The look on Ramon's face was the most priceless. He didn't expect her to know the difference. We all lost it." Kiergen was still laughing, two years later.

Isidora chuckled politely, shaking her head. "No, I've never heard that story. Poor Cinnia."

"Lucky Henri. But now I have to know, have you done the kiss test? Did you pass?"

"I'll pass on doing the test! Cinnia would punch *me*."

"Ha! Perhaps you're right." Kiergen was plainly disappointed, though. He asked after Cinnia and Henri, then moved on, leaving them alone.

Ramon watched Isidora's head bob lightly in time to the beat as she sipped the last of her drink. He was about to ask her to dance when she said, "I did, though."

"Did what?"

She kept her eyes on the dancers, speaking just loudly enough for him to hear her over a song about loving cheap thrills. "I kissed Henri."

It was time to switch to water. She kept working up a thirst on the dance floor, then draining gin-and-tonics. That was her third. Fourth? If she was losing count, it was definitely time to switch. Also her tongue was getting way too loose if she was starting to think that baiting her fiancé was a good idea.

Perhaps he thought so, too, because he plucked her glass out of her hand and gave it to his guard, then caught her elbow and spun her a few steps, pulling her behind a heavy curtain.

"What…where—?" She had thought the drapes decorative, but they disguised alcoves where chairs were stacked. The towers at the back reached to the ceiling, while others sat two and three high near where they stood crowded into the small space at the front.

"When?" he demanded, hands firm on her upper arms.

She automatically brought her hands to his chest and— Oh. Her fingers splayed against the firm heat of his chest, instinctively wanting to feel as much of his muscled torso beneath fine linen as possible.

"Isidora. When did you kiss Henri?"

Her light press into his chest was no match for his strength. He drew her closer so his mouth brushed the hair near her ear, causing a frisson of tickling sensation all the way down her neck and farther to the base of her spine. "Tell me."

"I don't know." How was she supposed to think, surrounded by his masculine scent like this? Ever since that moment at the flat, she'd been wondering if she had imagined the flash of carnal heat in him. She knew it had happened on her side, but him?

I've always thought you were beautiful.

He was such a liar! He hadn't even known she was alive. Still didn't.

Did he?

"Since Cinnia?"

"No. Long before. I was visiting Trella at Sus Brazos." She threw back her head, but it was nearly impossible to see him in the thin sliver of light that came in over the top of the drapes from the dimly lit ballroom. "I wasn't at university yet."

"Are you serious?" His hands tightened on her arms. "And he kissed you? Or did you kiss him?"

She wanted to kiss *him*.

Oh, she was sorry she'd been drinking. All her defenses were slipping away like scarves off an exotic dancer. Her body wanted to sway and slither against him. *Come hither, virile man.* She really was just like her mother.

And deep down, despite her continued lectures against that silly child who had been so infatuated, she wanted to believe that he did, indeed, think she was beautiful.

She wanted to prove it. She wanted to bring him to his knees with lust and adoration.

"Why does it matter?" she asked, nudging her nose against his stubbled jaw, feeling his hands flex on her arms and finding it erotic to be trapped in his hold like this. Since when did she have a kink for restraint?

"It matters. How old were you exactly?"

"I don't know." She grew a little drunker as she realized how invested he was. She couldn't resist taunting. "Sixteen?"

His grip tightened to just short of painful. "Which would have made him twenty-four. I'll kill him."

She smiled at how incensed he was. "Relax," she chided. "It was my idea. I came up to him like this." She shifted enough to feel his stubble graze her lips. She stepped in so her arms looped up behind his neck and her body brushed his. "*He* didn't scream when I did this…"

She went onto tiptoes so she was leaning against the taut line of his body and pressed her mouth to his, vaguely remembering the feel of a warm mouth that had parted with a smile, not anything resembling passion or reciprocation.

"I'm not Ramon," Henri had said, gently but promptly easing her back onto her feet. "And I'm not going to tell him, if that's what you're hoping. But thank you. That was very nice."

It had been a very adolescent move, both an attempt to prompt Henri to tell Ramon, hopefully inciting possessiveness, and an exploration of her feelings for the wrong twin. The peck had amounted to a Christmas kiss. Henri had essentially patted her on the head and told her to go play. Only the compassion in his eyes had kept the moment from being completely humiliating.

Ramon didn't express humor at the touch of her mouth. Or stop her.

He slid his arms around her so they banded across her back and held her in place as he stole control of their kiss.

She might have groaned as his mouth crushed hers. It was impossible to hear over a song blaring about not being able to stop the feeling.

A shudder of relief went through her as he slaked a thirst she'd suffered for years. It was not unlike falling into bed after a long day. Like tasting a rich dessert as it melted on her tongue.

Like kissing a man she had always found insanely attractive.

Don't *do* this, she warned herself, but couldn't resist. He kissed like the expert he was and his abundant skill made her furious enough, jealous enough, to kiss him back without inhibition. In silence, using only the rock of her mouth beneath his and the spear of her tongue into his mouth, she mused, *Feel that, Ramon?*

She *was* beautiful. In that moment, she was confident in her attraction. Arrogant. Other men came on to her. They were going crazy for her tonight. Why not him? He didn't know what he was missing. This. This is what he could have had all this time, if he had only asked.

She dug her fingers into his hair to draw him down and pressed her mouth more firmly to his. She stroked her tongue against his and groaned again, unreservedly, strong enough he must have felt the vibration in her throat. Arching her back, she rubbed her breasts against his chest, following the beat in the music that throbbed around them.

Their kiss became a dirty dance. He dropped his hand to her backside and firmly snugged her hips into his, working with the pulse of the song. His other hand brushed aside the front of her jumpsuit so he claimed her bare breast, his palm hot. He splayed his fingers and massaged, tongue stabbing against hers.

He was hard.

Mind blown, she rocked her hips between his firm caress of her cheek and the ridge of flesh that proved he found her desirable. That reaction in him ought to make her feel superior. She should have pushed away at that point to give him a scathing and triumphant "ha!"

But the allure of rubbing against him was too much. The tips of her breasts ached. Her loins felt hollow and needy. She couldn't resist staying exactly where she was, moving against him in time to the music.

He kept her against him as he turned and shuffled backward, drawing her down as he sat. She flowed weakly, like she was under a spell, more than happy to let him pull her astride his lap as he lowered into a chair. Both his wide hands slid to her lower back and cupped her butt to pull her hard against his fly.

A flash of sensation went through her, so sharp she threw back her head and let out a gasp, seeing nothing but shadows moving on the ceiling, as dark and mysterious as the sensations that flowed through her.

That moment might have given her pause, but he kissed her throat. He cupped her breast and plumped it again, dipping his head to bite gently at the upper swell, then flicked her nipple with his tongue.

She arched, wanting that tease, but wanting to rock herself against that hard ridge between her legs.

His hand on her hip urged her to move against his fly, to take up the rhythm of the song again, while he pinched her nipple and lifted his head to kiss her once more.

At the edges of her consciousness, she knew this was filthy. They were practically in public. He must have snuck behind a thousand curtains with other women, given how quickly and easily he had lured her here.

But with her knees wide and her heeled shoes braced on the floor, *she* was the woman pressed sex-to-sex with him tonight. The only thing between them was a few layers of fabric and they might as well have been naked for all the dulling of sensation.

And she was mad at him. Mad *for* him.

Maybe she thought she could make him break first. She wasn't really examining her motives, just reacting to the pleasure of rubbing against him while being in the control position, riding his lap, driving him crazy.

"Do you like that?" She caught at his earlobe with her teeth, arms folded behind his neck, breasts mashed to his chest.

His fingers dug in to the seam that traced the cleft of her butt. He bit out a really graphic curse of agreement. "Keep going."

She faltered. He was hard all over. He had admitted he enjoyed what she was doing to him. Here was the point she should pull away and show him she could take him or leave him. If she kept going…

How far did he expect her to go?

He bared her other breast, the cool air erotic and dangerous. Stimulating. The brush of his fingers against her aching nipple sent a spark of acute need into her loins. Heat flooded into her chest, making her breasts feel fuller and more sensitive. Her sex grew needier. Greedier.

Instinct made her take up the rock against him again, or maybe it was his hand on her butt.

This was getting out of control. Either way, lightning streaked into the place between her legs.

She shifted her grip to the back of his chair while his flat hand against her tailbone kept her hips tight to his. He lifted into her, continuing to excite her as he caught her mouth in a kiss that was insanely wicked. His tongue sought hers as he practically made love to her fully clothed in that chair, lifting her higher into the cloud of acute arousal. Driving her toward climax.

She was a virgin, but she knew how to give herself an orgasm if she wanted one. She had never felt a strong need for a man to perform that duty, but here she was, legs splayed, encouraging the lethal thrust of his hips against her. It was primal and, damn, he knew exactly how to play against her button of nerves like a bow against strings.

She had no will to stop his pushing her toward the brink, loving everything he was doing to her, no longer caring where she was, only wanting *this*.

She wanted that rush, wanted to feel it here, in his arms. Ramon's arms. Ramon's hips rolling against hers until she quivered on the edge.

The tension grew so intense she tried to close her thighs, but she couldn't. She was at his mercy, the coil of desire pulling into unbearable need that made her catch back a sob.

She clutched the back of the chair and closed her teeth on his bottom lip, trying to fight the rising wave, but he palmed her breast and kept up the relentless lift of his hips against hers. Shivers went down her spine, making her shoulder blades flex. She arched as the tingle spread across her lower back, then poured like liquid pleasure through her loins and thighs.

Release shuddered through her in a rush of joy. Sexy, hungry pulses followed, making her grind against him with abandon, eager to wring every last clench of deliciousness from their encounter.

It was so good…so good.

And so solitary.

She felt the dry laugh that went through him. The hoarse sound could have been a saber, it rent her so badly.

She wilted into his caging arms, shaken and breathless. Defeated.

This man had possessed her attention for far too long and now owned what shreds of dignity she had managed to preserve.

This was the most humiliating encounter of her life.

And there was no coming back from it.

CHAPTER SIX

"Come here," Ramon said the second he closed the door of his flat.

He could barely speak and didn't even remember getting here. He vaguely recalled a quick exit through a service door and a brisk walk through a bustling kitchen to the underground car park. That sort of disappearing act was exactly what he paid his security service to provide.

All that mattered was that he had her alone now. Properly alone, where he could strip off that maddening jumpsuit and satisfy both of them this time. If she had been wearing a dress tonight… But she hadn't been and damn it, he was *aching* to finish what they'd started.

She sent him a baleful glance. "Where are the extra blankets? I'll take the sofa."

She clutched her sheer black wrap like it was a trench coat, her mouth clean of lipstick from their kisses, her eyes dark with betrayal.

"Qué?" His voice came out harsher than he intended as he clung to something he could see was already moving beyond his reach, even before she spoke again.

"I told you I wouldn't sleep with you."

Then she had lap-danced him into believing she wanted to. She had come apart in his arms with such abandon, he'd nearly exploded. His heart was still thudding, hammering an obsessive pulse in the stiff flesh between his thighs.

Want. Need. *Have.*

But the wariness in her expression put the brakes on that. He firmly believed in a woman's right to change her mind, but he searched her expression, trying to understand how they had gone from ecstasy to aversion in a five-minute car ride. It put his lungs in a vise.

"Why did you say you wanted to leave, then?"

I want to go. The crack in her voice and the final twitch of postclimax that had shivered through her as she'd sat up, pressing her weight into his straining flesh, had been all the excuse he'd needed for a very swift and wordless departure from his own party.

"I couldn't face people after that!" She hugged herself, eyes wide and appalled.

"Dios," he muttered, not expecting her to be shy about it. "No one knew what we were doing. They didn't even know where we were."

"Oh, please." Her fingertips were digging so hard into her upper arms, she was going to leave bruises. "Everyone wants to know where you are and what you're doing at all times. I guarantee someone was watching and that your friend Kiergen will be adding this to his roster of stories. 'Remember that time Ramon pulled his fiancée behind the curtain for a blowie?'"

"Well, he'll be wrong, won't he?" Her crude talk didn't bother him so much as the fact she might be right. But he had had to become inured to gossip long ago. "*Who cares* what people say? We know the truth. That's all that matters."

"I care! And the truth isn't any more palatable." She let out a choked laugh. "I criticize you for not being able to share a night with a woman, but I can't even share a chair." She hung her head into her palm.

"We are *not* still fighting about your mother." His teeth came together and the rest came out between them. "I didn't have sex with her. Believe me this time because I'm not going to say it again." Inside his pocket, his hand closed into a fist.

She averted her face, but he watched her profile struggle with anger and a despair that made his chest feel tight.

"Whether you did or not doesn't matter. I'm sure you're both well over it by now. But I'm not like that, okay? I don't sleep around. I don't have sex in public. *I'm not like her*, Ramon."

Ah, hell.

"I know you're not like her," he said more gently.

Her head came up to send him a look of misery. "Judging by tonight's performance, are you?"

Which is when he realized this wasn't a case of self-consciousness or embarrassment, but shame. Deep shame. Her face was an agonized red, the corners of her mouth dragged with disgrace. She wore the cloak of someone who didn't know how to hide from herself.

"Don't." The word came out from deep in his chest, where a pressure settled, heavy as a piano. He couldn't bear that she regretted one of the most erotic and exciting experiences of his life. "Isidora—"

He started forward, but she retreated. Recoiled. She caught at the back of the chair that she bumped into, swaying before she gathered her excuse for a jacket around herself again.

A breath gusted out of him, leaving a hole in his chest.

"You know I'm not going to force you into anything. Don't you?" He was surprised his voice was so steady when he felt so flabbergasted.

"Except an engagement?"

"Sexually," he clarified. "You know enough about Trella's experience to believe me when I say I would never take advantage of a woman that way. That's why I was angry with you that morning at your mother's," he added with a return of ire. "You knew me. I was offended that you jumped so quickly to thinking I'd had sex with her."

"Oh, my fault! Silly me, making things up for no reason."

Dios. "All right, I know why you assumed I had—"

"No, you don't know!" Her jagged voice brimmed with acid.

He did. He had lived in Madrid on and off all his life. Gossip about her mother had always been rife.

"She had a rough childhood," he reminded her. "She told me that night how she'd been bounced between guardians, everyone fighting over her money and not giving a damn about her."

Francisca had married way too young and her first husband had abused her. The second had been too old, but had doubled her fortune when he died, turning her into the merriest of widows. By the time she had been pregnant with Isidora, not even thirty yet, she was entering her third marriage with Bernardo.

"If she was a man, no one would care how she conducts herself. People shouldn't judge her just because she's a woman. You shouldn't."

Her jaw dropped. "Don't you *dare* tell me how to feel about it! Did anyone ever ask you if your knees were as loose as your mother's? Were you ever refused service in a restaurant, in front of your friends, because your mother had slept with the owner's husband? How many times did you lie to your father about why a man was in the house, because you didn't want to hear another fight go on for days, and were afraid he would leave for good if he knew the truth?"

At the mention of her father, his chest grew too tight for his ribs, but he couldn't pile on her pain by telling her Francisca had confided to him that Bernardo wasn't her biological father.

"Isidora—"

"I don't tell you how to feel about your past, do I?" Her hands flung through the air in agitation. "And for your information, I *don't* judge her. I don't care how many men she sleeps with. I care that she's hurting so badly she can't stop herself. I care that I can't fix her. I care that men take advantage of her and people say things behind her back that only hurts her more."

"Well, I didn't take advantage of her," he growled. "We *talked. Bueno*? About *my* past. It was the anniversary of my father's death, Isidora. It pisses me off that you've never figured that out, which I know isn't fair, but you know everything about me. I didn't feel I should have to tell you. I didn't want to be alone that night and your mother was the perfect companion. She knew Mama from their boarding-school days. Papa had managed her trust from the time she had access to it. She talked about their wedding day. Told me stories I'd never heard, from when they were young and happy. From before." Before Trella's kidnapping, he meant. "Don't begrudge me that. I needed it."

She stared at him, motionless but for the throb of the artery in her throat.

"It's the truth," he said, trying to impress it through her brain, *needing* her to believe it.

"Then why…?" The profound hurt in her eyes twisted up his insides. "Why didn't you just tell me that?"

"Because I was angry." Tempted. Stung. He shook off the confusion that had driven him that morning. The sudden want as he'd realized she was a grown woman and the sight of the dead end they were doomed to hit. "Nothing was ever going to happen between us. You're the daughter of my father's friend. My sisters' friend. Was I supposed to lead you on? Date you and dump you? *Marry* you? I'm never going to marry anyone and *you*, in this position of having threats online and a damn army protecting you because of *me*, have to understand why I say that. So tell me, Isidora. What the hell was I supposed to do about that damn crush of yours except kill it so you could get on with your life?"

She sucked in a breath as though it was the last one she would ever take.

After a moment, she swallowed loud enough for him to hear. The glow that was brimming on her lashes threatened to spill onto her cheeks.

"So what was tonight? Pity? Throw a bone to the girl who used to love you?" Her brow flinched in acute humiliation.

"No." His ears hung up on *used to* while the rest of him tried to figure out what it *had* been. Sex didn't have hidden meanings for him, but even he knew it hadn't been the sort of quid pro quo he usually engaged in. The idea of her kissing his twin had set something alight in him. The sense of competition that had come over him had been the least friendly he'd ever felt toward Henri. It had been downright savage. Territorial.

That's what had driven him to kiss her, at least. A completely uncharacteristic possessiveness had gripped him as he'd held her, making him want to erase thoughts of any other man from her mind and replace them with himself.

Lust had taken over. She'd been so responsive—her breasts were perfection, her weight on him pure seduction, her abandonment to their lovemaking completely enthralling. He was a very experienced man, yet he would never forget something that amounted to adolescent petting behind the bleachers.

"You kissed me. I thought it meant you were willing to settle for an affair." It sounded lame even to his ears. He wasn't surprised she only shook her head.

"Maybe I would, if I thought you wanted *me*, and not just the woman you were stuck with because of this stupid engagement."

"I want you." How could she doubt it? "Look in a mirror. Of course I think you're beautiful. Of course I want to sleep with you."

"Because I'm *here*. Not because I'm *me*." She pointed to where her pendant hung against her bare breastbone. It swung forward as she leaned into her words. "In the entire time I've known you, you've never treated me as anything but a giant pain in your behind. Henri used to at least have a conversation with me, but not you."

She pointed at him to punctuate.

"I was that thing you had to endure coming into your house because I happened to be friends with your sisters. Then you did me this great favor of shattering my heart by appearing to sleep with my *mother*."

She straightened, shoulders back, chin up.

"Five *years* go by and do you *ask* me to help with your sister? No! You threatened my job and pressed on my loyalty to your family. And now, after all of that, I'm supposed to fall down with gratitude that the great Ramon Sauveterre has decided I'm physically attractive enough that he's *inviting* me to have an affair? Thanks a bunch."

This time, her hostility didn't grate. That vilification

clawed past his thick skin to the center of his soul, which he suddenly feared was a vacant space. She'd pulled back the curtain, pointed and made him feel small. Dishonorable.

"So that's a no, then?" He took refuge behind sarcasm because no one was supposed to be able to hurt him. Not this badly. Not by holding him up to the light and finding such an ugly angle.

He feared the rasp in his voice gave away what a direct hit she'd scored, but she only widened her gray eyes in disbelief. Then she shook her head like she should have expected his callousness.

"When I was young, I used to think your past made you afraid of being hurt. I told myself that's why you wouldn't love me back. It made the rejection easier. But you're actually just a self-important, unfeeling bastard, aren't you? Here's news. Some people react to life's tragedies by being nice. They try to make the world a better place. They don't ruin it for everyone else. I will never forgive you for forcibly dragging me back to your side so you could teach me again that you're not worth my time."

She turned toward the bedroom, one wrist coming up so she could use her sleeve against her cheek.

"Isidora."

"Really?" she cried. "I have to spell it out?" She kept her back to him. "That was a hard no, Ramon. Step outside if you want sex. I'm sure you can flag some down with that charm of yours. I'm going to have a bath and sleep on the sofa."

"Take the bed. I have some calls to make."

"So noble."

As he heard the tub faucet start, he moved to the cabinet in the lounge and poured himself a strong start on a terrible hangover.

* * *

They both wore sunglasses the next morning. Isidora was trying to hide that she had cried—yes, again—over that stupid man.

She didn't know what was up with Ramon, though. She didn't think he'd had that much to drink at the party, but he informed her flatly that he had called in their regrets for a brunch they were supposed to attend. He had a tall cup of the coffee she'd made, but didn't touch any of the pastries she had sent up.

That suggested an unsteady stomach. She noted a near-empty bottle of Scotch on the end table in the lounge as he moved into the shower she'd vacated, but she didn't ask.

She wouldn't spare one word in his direction if she didn't have to.

And she personally wouldn't touch alcohol again for a long time. She was still writhing internally at how she had behaved. The part where she had climaxed on his lap was bad enough, but then she had bared her soul and he had only scoffed at her history of unrequited love like it was a skinned knee.

The next few months were going to be interminable.

As if to prove it, they met Kiergen in the lobby as they were leaving. Apparently he had a flat in the building, too.

"Where did you two get off to? As if I didn't know," he said with a playful leer.

Before Isidora could smile weakly through her squirming blush, Ramon said bluntly, "A personal matter came up."

Kiergen's smile gave way to concern. "I hope everything is all right? Are you still coming to the brunch?"

"No. Excuse us. The car is waiting." He hurried her

out, leaving Kiergen sounding worried as he called out a wish that they travel safe.

As they settled into the cool leather seats and the car pulled way, she glanced briefly at Ramon. He really was a master class in manipulating his own image. Now Kiergen would go to the brunch with genuine concern over this "personal matter." Speculation would abound, and no one would be aware it was pure red herring.

Was she supposed to thank him for covering up her lunacy?

She churlishly chose to read emails instead, doing her best to ignore him while feeling slighted that he did the same.

They had a milk run of business engagements for the next few days, crisscrossing to Italy and Germany before coming back to France. She was mostly arm candy at luncheons and cocktail parties as he shook hands and took photos with newly promoted executives.

It was nice to see a mix of women taking management positions and the conglomerate wasn't named Sauveterre *International* for nothing. At least it gave her a broad range of people to chat with as a buffer against him.

They were able to avoid all but the bare minimum of physical contact, too. If they kissed, it was a perfunctory performance—not unlike the kiss she had exchanged with his brother, if distinctly less warm. And while they smiled at each other when they had to, they spoke as little as possible.

It was a delicate balance on the edge of a razor blade, cutting into her relentlessly as they crawled along with this charade.

So, even though she was loath to be without external distractions to keep them apart, it was a relief to board his yacht to sail across the Mediterranean to Málaga,

Spain, where their official engagement party would be held.

To the long-lens cameras spying on them from afar, they appeared to be on a prehoneymoon. In reality, Ramon worked tirelessly from his onboard office. She answered emails and wrote press releases while sunbathing in her bikini. They saw each other over meals and confined conversation to work-related topics.

One day, she kept promising herself, she would be over Ramon and would fall for a man who adored her. Their passion would overshadow that bit of petting she had shared with Ramon. They would marry in a dream wedding, have a handful of children and this gnawing ache inside her would subside.

But that was many days away. She still had half of *this* day to get through.

She gave the purser a brief thank-you smile as she took her seat across from Ramon at lunch. He wore a collared short-sleeved shirt and casual shorts with deck shoes. She had shrugged on a simple red sundress over her bathing suit since they were eating poolside.

"Did you see that email about—"

"Yes. I told them not to bother."

It was exactly the minimum exchange they had been keeping to for days. Was he sulking because she had refused to sleep with him? She might think so if he wasn't so completely unmoved.

He was back to ignoring her the way he had most of her life. It stung. She didn't expect an apology. He was hardly the type to go that far, but she would prefer anger, if that's what he felt. Some kind of emotion. This stiff politeness was horrible. And why did it make her feel like she was at fault? Was it a woman thing?

She bit back a sigh and declined a glass of wine.

Taking her cue from him, she picked up the phone she had set aside. It was pinging with a notification anyway. Before she could read it, Ramon let loose a string of sharp curses.

"What?" she prompted, sensing disaster and hurrying to unlock her screen.

Ramon saved her the trouble by turning his phone so she could read the alert Etienne had just sent.

This English translation just hit. It's been circulating in Arabic for an hour. The queen mother of Zhamair is quoted as stating her future daughter-in-law was not the twin in the photo kissing the Prince of Elazar last spring. True? How do I respond?

Trella still hadn't publicly confirmed or denied her pregnancy. Now she was exposed as having been with one of the most sought-after bachelors in Europe, one who was rumored to be on the brink of an engagement to someone else. Isidora had been doing her job, keeping up with online gossip about the prince. She'd been secretly worried for her friend. If he married while he already had a child coming with Trella, that would be disastrous!

She blew out a dismayed breath. "There's no pretending Kasim's mother is not a creditable source, is there? I mean, I've always wondered why Kasim allowed people to think Angelique had been with both him and the Elazar prince, but why would his mother go on record with such an inflammatory statement?"

"Kasim kept quiet because Gili asked him to. That smudge on her reputation is the reason they haven't announced their engagement. His highest-ranking advisors made it clear they wouldn't accept her as queen. My guess is that his mother chose to repair Gili's reputation by annihilating Trella's. I've met her. She takes things into her own hands without a sense of consequence." He was furious. She could hear it in his voice.

"I'll tell Etienne we're handling it." She began texting.

Ramon's phone buzzed and he swore again, then hitched his chair around to her side of the table, so they sat side by side and could both see his screen. She tingled with awareness at how close he suddenly was, but the message coming through from his sister was so shocking, it demanded her complete attention.

Apparently I'm married.

Angelique attached a breaking news story that contained a brief video of Kasim. He exited a closed-door meeting to be confronted with the storm surrounding his mother's statement. Reporters were demanding he respond to whether he intended to marry Angelique. Surely not, given all this controversy.

His reaction, released minutes ago, was already going viral.

Isidora had only met Kasim once. He would have intimidated the heck out of her even without the title of king of Zhamair. He was tall and dynamic. The only things remotely soft about him were his long-lashed, dreamy dark eyes. They were especially heart-melting when his gaze rested on Angelique.

The rest of him was short beard, desert garb and an uncompromising air. His essence of supreme power came through even on the small mobile screen as he spoke in Arabic, his implacable words translated as English subtitles beneath his unyielding image.

"Let me resolve this once and for all. *We are married.* I am king. If I say she is my wife, she is my wife. Treat her with the respect my queen deserves. Gossip and speculation will not be tolerated. Move on." He walked away.

Oh. She couldn't help the small chortle that pushed into the back of her throat. That was one way to handle it.

A quick flick to the social sites on her own phone showed the video was already looped to a GIF meme and beginning to trend. *If I say she is my wife...*

"So much for worrying about an engagement announcement." Isidora used a weak laugh to cover how envious she was. Kasim's defense of Angelique was ruthless and sexist, sure, but swoon-worthy.

Ramon immediately placed a video-chat call to his sister. Angelique appeared next to Trella, with their office at the design house in the background.

"Wait," Angelique said breathlessly. "Henri wants in." She tapped and added his image to the screen.

Ramon's twin held an infant swaddled in a pink blanket. Henri's jaw was shadowed in stubble, exactly like Ramon's. Their mother sat on one side of Henri, Cinnia sat on the other. Cinnia had a blanket draped over her shoulder, presumably nursing their second newborn. Cinnia looked tired, but healthy and happy as she said a warm "Congratulations!"

"Thank you." Angelique wiped at the tears tracking to the corners of her smiling mouth. "That's not the way we meant to do it. He just...said it. He's not the least bit sorry and neither am I."

She sighed, but it was a blissful one. Then she fanned her streaming eyes. "I don't know why I'm crying. I'm *happy.* And relieved. His mother was trying to override resistance to our engagement. She wanted to start planning the wedding, but now it's done. I'm married!" Her hands went up in bemusement.

"So no proper wedding?" their mother asked with a disappointed throb in her voice. "Henri's was in the hospital. I was so looking forward to a big affair with yours, Gili."

"We'll plan something, Mama," Angelique promised. "But right now a plane is waiting. I'm flying to Zhamair as soon as I throw a few things in a bag, but—"

She looked to Trella, who drew her in for a warm hug, then dried her sister's cheek with a gentle touch. "Our leaky little Gili is married. Don't worry about me. Go. Pack. Be with your husband."

Angelique was obviously torn. She looked to the screen as she rose. "Kasim's team will take care of my PR going forward. I hate to leave you all in the lurch—"

"You're not," everyone said in unison, making her laugh-cry again. "I love you all *so much*."

"We'll issue a statement that we're very happy for you," Ramon said. "Which we are. Will you come to the engagement party this weekend?"

"I have no idea. Kasim said something about honey-mooning at his oasis." She blushed. "Either way, you'll all come see me soon?"

"Count on it," Henri promised, which was quite an offer considering he literally had his hands full. As if on cue, the daughter he held began to fuss. He exchanged a rueful look with his wife. "Time to switch out again. We have to go. But Trella—"

She bowed her head against her hand. "I *know*."

"I've got this," Ramon said to his brother. "Take care of your *chicas*. *Besos*, Mama."

His mother blew them a kiss and Spain signed off. Angelique walked away, presumably to pack. Trella lifted her face from her hand. She sighed as she looked at her brother through the small screen. "Don't start."

"*Is* the prince of Elazar the father?" he asked. "Have you told him?"

"No."

"No, he's not the father? Or no, you haven't told him?"

She skipped past clarifying. "For Kasim's sake, Isidora can confirm that I was the twin in the photo. Hold off on announcing the pregnancy. I don't want to link the two in people's minds."

"Trella," Ramon growled.

"I'm handling this!"

"You're not. A baby doesn't go away, *hermana.*"

"Oh, you think? You're just mad I'm not letting *you* handle it."

"Trella," Isidora interjected. Once these two started arguing they could go on for days. She had heard it with her own ears. "Do I say whether the prince knew it was you? Is he likely to comment one way or another?"

Trella dug her hands through her hair, and groaned, "Don't say. We'll see if he comments and deal with it if he does."

"That's hardly 'handling it,' is it?" Ramon said. "The more you play coy, the worse this will get. I will—"

"What?" Trella challenged. "Make out with Izzy on the bow of the boat? Let them catch her topless? *Stop trying to fix this.* You *can't.* It's *my* problem, Ramon." She ended the call without another word.

With a feral noise, Ramon gripped his phone tightly and gave it a small shake. *"Braguillas."* Brat. He made a noise of disgust and set down the phone with a clatter.

Isidora scratched her upper lip. "Just to be clear, we're not, um, going to do those things, are we? I get to keep my top on?"

His gaze flicked across like a whip, his expression fierce. "Do you honestly think I would expect that of you?"

That arrogant tone got under her skin.

"I don't know, do I?" In the back of her mind, she knew she was deliberately provoking him, looking for any sort of reaction beyond flat disinterest. "It's something you *would* do. You always deflect attention from her. That's how I wound up in this fake engagement, if you recall."

She reached for her phone as a small shield, tensing with apprehension that he would come back with something about her chest not being enough to interest anyone.

His thundering silence was worse.

CHAPTER SEVEN

THIS WOMAN. SHE was driving him insane, revealing exactly what kind of fire burned inside her before tearing him down and locking him out.

The things she had revealed the night of the party had been a shock, and he hadn't dealt with it well in the moment, had been too sexually frustrated to process all that she had revealed—and how much shame she had sent crawling up inside him. But he'd had plenty of time for self-castigation since.

He had underestimated her feelings for him over the years, thinking them superficial because from the time he had become sexually active, he'd been treated as a trophy. Even the racing fans who "preferred" him over his brother were more interested in the driver than the man. Besides, Isidora hadn't been mature enough for anything more than surface infatuation, he had always believed.

But he couldn't stop hearing her say *"if I thought you wanted me."* Like she believed herself interchangeable with the women he'd encountered over the years.

She wasn't. Deep down, he had always known an affair with Isidora would be the furthest thing from impersonal. That's why he had held her off so uncompromisingly. Emotional intimacy made him close up inside.

He had told himself he was protecting *her*, denting her

ego, not her heart, but he wasn't so devoid of conscience he would pimp her out with topless photos, and it wasn't just because the idea of any man seeing her naked was abhorrent to him.

Really abhorrent.

"No, I wouldn't ask you to strip down to divert attention from my sister," he stated, biting out each word. "Effective as that might be."

She took up her fork and dipped her head, brows pulling with consternation as though she wasn't sure whether he was complimenting her or what.

It struck him afresh that his discouragement over the years had affected her far more seriously than he had intended. Looking back, he could see that a young woman's confidence could be impacted by such things, but at the time— He sighed with self-disgust.

"I shouldn't have taken advantage of your loyalty as badly as I have. I know what a precious commodity it is. Anyone else would have sold us out, or pushed me into traffic by now."

"If the doors to the terrace had been open the other night…" She stuffed a cherry tomato into her mouth, sealing her lips over the threat she didn't finish. But even as she chewed, he saw the faint tremble in her lips. His few words of culpability affected her.

He wasn't someone who apologized, and barely had just now, but she was moved. In that moment, he understood, really understood, what kind of power he had over her.

Maybe he had always known, because he tensed even now, wanting to turn away. He had the intelligence to know that the flip side of a power coin was responsibility. He already carried a lot of obligations. He didn't want more.

But there she perched, teetering in the place between his conscience and his sense of duty, whether he wanted to accept her presence or not. Something unsteady see-sawed in his chest, making him look to the horizon, hoping it was only the yacht listing on the waves.

He heard her draw a breath as though preparing to say something, but when he looked back at her, he saw hesitation. A change of mind.

"What?" he prompted.

"Nothing." She pushed at the greens on her plate with the tines of her fork. "I know that my loyalty is both my strength and my weakness, that's all."

That hadn't been what she had been about to say, he was sure of it, but now he wondered if that was why she hadn't pushed her mother out of her life, despite how much anguish Francisca's actions had caused her. Her mother was still keeping a secret that could devastate her, he recalled, and wished like hell he didn't know about it. If she ever found out he knew and hadn't told her, she really would push him into traffic.

"For instance, my loyalty to Trella demands that I ask why you're still playing human shield for her, even though I know you'll say it's not my place to ask."

"I do take a zero-tolerance approach to discussing my family." He felt like an ass as he said it, especially when she nodded, as if he had behaved as expected, but still slid her attention sideways to hide that she was stung.

"Even though I'm directly affected in this case." Her voice quavered with emotion. "I mean, I know you and Henri have reason to be protective, and I know she was hiding her panic attacks from the press. That's why she stayed out of the public eye all those years, but she has that under control now, right? So after all those years of her struggling to get a handle on things, she's finally ready to steer her own life. Why don't you want to let her? Why go the route of keeping me here, doing this? Don't say it's because she'll make mistakes. We all kiss frogs on the way to growing up."

Like him?

She cleared her throat, not meeting his gaze, but her chin took on a haughty angle. "For what it's worth, I agree with you. I think the prince is the father and that she should tell him. But it's not my life and it's not yours, either." "So there" was heavily implied.

She dropped her gaze to the face of her phone, chin set with belligerence, but he had the distinct feeling she was sitting there braced for a blast.

His knee-jerk reaction was to not just nip that sort of intrusion in the bud, but yank it out by the roots.

Yet here he sat, using a woman who only wanted to defend his sister. On the brink of hurting Isidora again, because she dared ask why he was using *her*.

The fluttering snap of the flag at the stern filled the silence.

"Whatever," she muttered, shoving aside her plate. "I'll chalk it up to that childish contrariness you two have been locked in all your lives and get back to doing my 'job.'"

She started to rise.

"I've been called a lot of things. 'Childish' is not one of them."

"But you're willing to own 'contrary?'"

He curled his lip, not exactly warm to the idea, even though there was some truth to it. He and Trella *were* contrary. If he said black she had to say white. To this day, his little sister would always claim "*he* started it," even though she invariably picked their fights.

"I don't have brothers and sisters. I've never understood why you fight so much. I've always thought you two were lucky to have each other and should be nicer. Especially—"

She didn't finish, but he knew what she meant. He *was* lucky to have Trella, considering how close they had come to losing her.

"I don't fully understand it, either," he admitted, not sure if he was relieved or dismayed when Isidora let her hands and napkin fall back into her lap as she stayed to listen. "Henri has the patience to deal with Trella being headstrong and impulsive. Gili is so sensitive, she cries if they disagree. With me, Trella seems to challenge every single thing I say. There's six years between us. I don't antagonize her for the sake of it, but she has never accepted that I might know a few things."

Isidora's brows went up. She set her elbow on her armrest and propped her chin on her fist, wearing an expression of polite interest, but she rolled her lips inward to suppress a smile.

"Why is that funny?"

"I'm just wondering how much you know about being pregnant? By accident. By a prince."

He let out a heavy breath, *hating* this, but supposed he owed her an explanation.

"I left her to deal with her own problems once before. It didn't work out well." He moved his gaze to the endless horizon of blue on blue, holding that blankness inside him so he didn't have to deal with the roiling emotions beneath the surface.

"Ramon! No, you didn't." Her touch settled on his wrist, her fingertips cool against his skin, far more profound than her voice. He found himself holding very still, not wanting to startle her into lifting her hand and removing that tentative contact.

"Don't ever blame yourself for not catching up to that van before they got away."

"I'm not talking about the kidnapping." They'd all had therapy ad nauseam after Trella was recovered. He knew in his head he wasn't responsible for Trella's kidnapping. Gili's math tutor was. Ramon had been fifteen, a top athlete, and had chased the van until he collapsed with exhaustion. He still had sick moments when he went over and over that memory, thinking *maybe* and *if only*.

Therapy could only accomplish so much, but for the most part they had all put that trauma into the past. They had still been coming to terms with the rest, however, when Trella had been pulled into a fresh hell and they had all been sucked in with her.

"I mean later," he clarified, using the measured, disembodied voice he used when he had no choice but to go back to the dark times. "After our father died."

He had the unnatural urge to turn up his palm and invite her hand to slip into his grip, but tensed against needing support. He *needed* to be strong, because as much as Trella exasperated him, she was also deeply vulnerable. He had to be a pillar for her. For all his family. Impervious.

"Grief isn't something you can fix for anyone." He could hear the confusion in her voice. "All you can do is be there and I know you were. Weren't you? I know you were racing…"

"I took time off from racing after Papa died. Henri and I were dealing with…*everything*. Grief. The board. They refused to hand the keys to the castle to a pair of new adults still wet behind the ears. Henri was going through our father's records, doing the sort of tedious work I can't stand. I was doing what I could to support Mama and the girls. Trella and Gili were supposed to start back at school, but Trella kept making excuses. Things were happening online that she didn't tell us about. Emails. Photographs and sexual harassment. Things that make me sick as a grown man. You can imagine what they did to a teenage girl with Trella's history."

She absorbed that in a beat of thoughtful silence, then murmured, "I always wondered why she was so adamant against starting social-media accounts. Is that what started her panic attacks?" Her hand stayed on his arm, was soothing despite just resting the light weight of her fingertips against his skin.

"Gili was getting the same messages, but neither of them wanted to worry us. She knew something was up with Trella, though. That it was worse for her. I kept saying she was just being Trella. Moody and obstinate. She had made so much progress since the kidnapping, I didn't see—I didn't *want* to see—that she was falling apart. Going past rock-bottom and not coming back. Like if I ignored it, I could keep it from happening."

He wanted to go back and shake that ignorant young man he'd been. If he had listened to Gili, if he had pushed past Trella's insistence that she was *fine*…

"She was supposed to come watch one of my races and changed her mind at the last minute. We argued and she told me to leave her alone. I took her at her word. It was the worst possible thing I could do."

He thought he heard Isidora's breath catch in apprehension, but he was lost in that awful moment of fearing that history had repeated itself.

"Gili was hysterical even before we got home, convinced something was wrong. We walked in the house and Trella was gone. I called the police, then checked the security footage. That's how I figured out where to look.

She was curled up in the back of her closet, biting a towel to keep from screaming, soaked with sweat."

"Oh, Trella," Isidora whispered, and moved her hand from his arm to cover her heart. "There were so many times when I would ask if I could come see her and she would say it wasn't a good day. I had no idea it was ever *that* bad."

"No one but family does." He looked around, realized where he was, but no one was on deck except the two of them. Perspiration coated his back as he leaned forward, letting the breeze ripple his shirt and pull him back to the present.

"I would never tell anyone."

"I know." He was still impatient with himself. "I shouldn't have said anything regardless. It's her secret to tell, not mine. I wish I could say that was the worst of it, but those same panic attacks happened again and again, sometimes as night terrors, other times hours straight of racing heart and deep anxiety. She didn't get them under control until she pulled out of the public eye completely. Even then, it's been a long haul to get here. We're all holding our breath and is she keeping a low profile, taking things slow? Hell, no. Not Trella." He flung up an exasperated hand. "She's sleeping with strangers, getting pregnant by a damn prince who has his own publicity nightmare to manage. That is why, *cariño*, I have forced you into the spotlight with me. I never want her to go through that again."

Ramon's tormented profile twisted her stomach into a knot.

In so many ways, this man had stolen her heart by being strong. The very first time she had ever seen him, he had picked her up off the grass at an executive picnic for Sauveterre International. She'd been five or six and he had set her on her feet like it was nothing, then called out to the boys who had rushed past and knocked her down that they should be more careful.

After the kidnapping, when her father had made house calls to his, she hadn't understood why her friends were so different, so sad. Even some of the grown-ups cried sometimes, but if Ramon or Henri wept, they did it behind closed doors.

By the time she had begun to stir with a more primal, feminine understanding of male strength, Ramon had been a godlike figure who dominated her imagination. He'd been a dynamic alpha who tamed a thousand horses with the pedals of one car. There were no contests he didn't win, no weights his broad shoulders couldn't carry.

In truth, she had set him up for a role he was too human to live up to.

No wonder he had pushed her away. Who needed that much pressure? He had enough on his plate conquering his personal demons.

But until this moment, she hadn't seen them. Not this closely. Not this nakedly.

She had sat with her hand on his arm while he had revealed the dark space inside himself. Now he had retreated into it and she wanted to respect that need for privacy, but more than anything, she wanted to pull him out of that grim place. There was no way to fix his bleak past, though. No way to guarantee bad things wouldn't happen in the future.

All she could do was let him know he was not alone in this moment. He had drafted her into the role of his fiancée. She loved his sisters and owed his family, so she was willing to continue this engagement, but she knew in her heart, she was doing it for his sake, too. Because she was who she was and she did want to make the world a better place, one tiny ray of light at a time.

"I *would* let myself be photographed topless—"

"Like hell." His head snapped around so fast, and his voice was so dour, that her heart clenched. It skipped at the same time, buoyed by a giddy urge to laugh.

She was such an idiot to think he was being protective, to like it, but she still grasped at it as she continued.

"To take the heat off this latest news about Trella."

"I said *no*."

"But we'd probably have more success if we pretended I dropped my engagement ring overboard."

His thunderous expression eased into a faint smirk.

"You're starting to think like me. I'm not sure that's a good thing." He nodded once. "Let's eat, then go fishing."

They managed an uneasy truce as they finished their travel into Málaga. Since they were the guests of honor at their engagement party, they stayed at the hotel where it was being held, rather than at Sus Brazos with the rest of his family.

The hotel was a completely refurbished nineteenth-century structure. All the five-star amenities had been added, but the rooms described as "charming" and "authentic" were actually "small" and "snug." Ramon had taken their best suite, but with their own guest list competing for rooms with wealthy vacationers from across Europe, he hadn't been able to take any extra space.

They were back to either sharing a bed or arguing, until he volunteered to take that torture device the decorator no doubt called "a delightful period piece." It looked no bigger than the average love seat and sported filigreed armrests.

Isidora gave the bed a circumspect glance and asked if he needed the bathroom before she started getting ready.

He nursed a Scotch on the balcony, watching the waves against the beach, trying not to think of that bed behind him. Yesterday he'd spent the afternoon lusting after her in a bikini as they'd spent a couple of hours diving for an engagement ring that was in the safe in his onboard office.

Damn it, if he wanted sex, Isidora was right. He didn't have to go very far. He turned down more offers than he accepted. Finding someone to discreetly take the edge off behind the back of his "fiancée" would not be difficult. But as he glanced over the topless, golden bodies wandering in from a day on the sand, he found himself turned off by the idea of a quick frolic with a stranger.

He wanted Isidora. Since that night in Monaco, he had been obsessively imagining bringing her to the same kind of shattering orgasm she'd had in his lap, but pumping into her while it happened, intimately feeling her contractions of ecstasy, finding his own pleasure at the same time.

Damn, but it was hot this summer!

With a soft curse, he drained his Scotch and chewed an ice cube, then moved into the air-conditioning, finding no relief as he changed into his tuxedo.

He had never been so preoccupied by a woman. It was uncomfortable. Especially when he wanted... He shook his head at himself. He wanted to be friends. When he had opened up about Trella, Isidora hadn't offered platitudes like "I understand," or "it will be all right." She had sat with her warm touch on his arm, waiting to lead him out of his own closet of fear.

That patient contact had been so profound it seemed to reach all the way to his heart. He had *felt* understood.

He couldn't ruin that tentative trust by asking her again for an empty affair.

Tying his bow tie, he heard a noise behind him and turned.

And swore.

Isidora was flawless in a black-velvet, one-shoulder gown that hugged her breasts and hips. It might have bordered on unremarkable if not for the faux diamonds that traced the shoulder strap and followed the cutout beneath her left breast, drawing the eye to where the creamy skin of her rib cage and waist was exposed.

He didn't want to just touch that bare skin, he wanted to feel the soft heat of it against his open mouth, taste it, feel her squirm under butterfly kisses and arch as he sucked.

"No?" Her hand went to her middle. "I have a red gown—"

"No. I mean yes. You have completely emptied my brain, woman." He ate up her slender arms, her upper chest, the flex in her throat as she swallowed. Her hair was gathered with a line of sparkling diamonds, exposing a blue stone dangling from her earlobe. "You look fantastic."

"Ramon—" Her shy face twisted into a drawn, anxious expression.

He hurried forward, like he could save something falling from a cart.

"That isn't flattery. I'm not being polite. You have never escaped my notice, Isidora. I wanted to ignore you. I *tried*. But even when you were just a chatty, flat-chested sprite of a thing, I couldn't overlook you."

He stopped her hands from wringing by taking them in his own.

"If I hurt you—" He swore. "I know I've hurt you."

He circled his thumb over the tip of her pointed knuckle, aware of the way her fingers fluttered against his loose grip, like a nervous bird's wings. "I'm sorry."

It surprised him how hard it was to say the words. A lot of remorse came with the admission, leaving a tightness in his chest that caused a scrape in his voice.

"Sometimes yours was the only laugh we heard in our house all week. It bothers me that I might have cut that off. I don't think I've heard you laugh since…"

Hell, probably since before her mother's lounge five years ago.

He closed his eyes in regret and brought her bent fingers to his lips, pressing his apology into them.

Her breath caught. The cool stone in her ring grazed near the corner of his mouth and the backs of his thumbs touched the prickle on his own chin. He grimaced, releasing her to rub at his stubbled jaw. "I should shave before I forget."

"You should." Her voice was thick with emotion. "Thank you, Ramon."

"For shaving?" He knew what she meant, but the moment was too charged for his liking. "I don't want you to be uncomfortable when we kiss at our party."

Completely leveled, Isidora tried to gather her composure.

I'm sorry. Such small words, spoken so quietly, but the impact was huge. Her throat felt swollen and her heart ran like a freight train in her chest.

When she heard him come back a few minutes later, she still couldn't look at him, too moved. Too overwhelmed. She checked that she hadn't chewed off her lipstick and swept out the door he held open for her. It wasn't until they were in the elevator with their guards that her gaze tracked to his in the mirror they faced.

"I thought you were going to shave?" He looked quite the ruffian in a tuxedo with that five o'clock shadow. Very devil-may-care. If he loosened his bow tie her knees would unhinge completely.

He made a face and scraped his palm against his cheek. "My razor broke."

"We could have one sent up. Do you want to go back?"

His guard, Oscar, extended a finger toward the panel.

"There's no point. I know what the problem is and something else will happen to stop me. Resistance is futile."

"What do you mean?" She turned from the reflection to the man. "I noticed you've been wearing stubble more often lately. I thought it was a fashion choice."

"A fashion choice," he repeated with a choked noise, clearly offended. "*No.* I'm not being lazy, either."

"What then?"

"I don't want to tell you. You'll laugh." His lip curled, but the way he eyed her sent rising bubbles of amusement into her chest.

She made a show of holding a bored expression and glancing at her nails. "I heard a rumor that was a goal of yours, but whatever…"

The doors opened to the lobby, putting an abrupt end to what had been the beginnings of very enjoyable, light-hearted flirting. The dull roar of conversation filled the space on the second floor, where a chandelier hung amid a gallery of masterpieces in gilded frames.

They stepped out and Ramon halted her with a touch on her arm.

"Come here, then." He veered her from the throng crowding the marble floor around the fountain and drew her into a small kiosk. It had probably held a telephone at one point, but now housed a terminal for airline check-ins and other online tasks.

It was close quarters. She brought her hands up to rest on his lapels, conscious of the hard wall of his chest.

"What, um—" She hadn't been this close to him since sitting astride him. The sting of a blush crept into her cheeks. She looked to the sliding door he had pulled closed behind them.

"It's new-father syndrome. I've seen it with our executives. They look like they're coming to work after a terrific bender, but it's just a fresh baby at home."

That surprised her into looking up with a confused frown. "Is there something you haven't told me?" She cocked her head. "Because I must say you're being very hard on your sister."

"Not me. My brother." He lightly cupped her elbows and his thumbs drew restless patterns against her skin, making a shiver run up her shoulders and into her chest, sensitizing her nipples. She tried to ignore it.

"You want me to believe that Henri is forgetting to shave so you are, too?" She shook her head. "The universe broke your razor?"

"Do you think we dress alike because we think it's cute?"

"You're businessmen. The uniform is a three-piece suit. Of course you'll grab the same white shirt now and again."

"And the same tie? And the same shoes?"

She shook her head. "I'm not as gullible as those people who think twins are psychic." Lowering her brow, she asked with suspicion, "*Are* you psychic?"

"No." Amusement played around his mouth.

He really had a beautiful mouth. The seam of his lips

was quite wide, but his upper lip was defined with two strong peaks, while his bottom lip was smooth and full, inviting a nibble.

"Isidora."

She'd never heard her name spoken in such a husky, sexy tone. When he cupped the side of her neck, she felt as though her body fell away. She became something ephemeral, pulse throbbing against the heat of his hand on her throat as his green, green eyes held her in thrall.

"You accused me of wanting you because you're convenient, but that is so far from the truth. My brain is telling me not to wreck the peace we've finally made, but I can't stop thinking about what we started. About how passionate you are. *You*. It's not convenient at all."

She grew hotter with every word. Beyond the door, one of the guards said something.

"I think someone wants in here," she said, desperate for escape before she did something stupid, like fall all over him again.

Ramon's hand dropped from her neck, leaving a chill that increased as he opened the door.

The indirect lighting against the yellowed facade of the hotel, along with the candles floating in the pool, cast a warm glow over the bricked area that had been roped off all the way to the beach. A string trio played for the reception portion, to be replaced by a livelier dance band after the champagne toast.

Paparazzi had already bribed their way into positions along the velvet rails and off some balconies, determined to snap photos of the celebrities Ramon had deliberately invited. He could have held the party in the privacy of Sus Brazos, but that ultrahigh security would have defeated the purpose. This party was the event of the year, intended to dominate the society pages so Trella wouldn't.

His sister arrived in a subtle maternity gown, choosing to let a picture speak a thousand words. Ramon sincerely hoped her plan to bury the news amid the spectacle of his engagement worked.

Letting go of his responsibility toward either of his sisters was easier said than done. At least Angelique was in good hands. Ramon had no doubt Kasim would die before allowing harm to come to her. He certainly had the resources to kill anyone who tried, but Ramon still did a quick scan to note where his sisters stood with their mother, a collective of guards on hand. Kasim, unruffled yet ever alert, stood at Angelique's side.

His shy little sister was a queen. Ramon still hadn't taken it in. Along with Henri and his babies, she now had too much responsibility to drop everything and rush to Trella's side when necessary. It was all on him.

The weight of that might have pushed him into grim introspection, but a sudden burst of laughter from Isidora yanked like a sweet hook in his heart. It wasn't just the tinkling sound that turned his head. He wanted to catch the way her eyes sparkled.

His breath stalled and he found himself smiling in reaction. Satisfaction and something more tender rolled through him. He hadn't destroyed that light in her after all.

"You knew!" she accused, squeezing his upper arm through his jacket and bumping into him at the same time, so he felt the press of her breast. "Did you call him?"

"Who?"

She waved at where Henri was coming toward them with Cinnia.

"Ah." It could be argued that all tuxedos looked alike,

that pleated shirts were de rigueur with one, but he and his brother both owned several penguin costumes. Despite that, he would bet their collective fortune that the same designer label was sewn into every article they both wore tonight. And Henri had *not* shaved.

They looked as they too often did—like mirror images. Their sisters regularly turned themselves out with individual looks unless they consciously chose to copy each other. Why the hell could he and Henri not manage it?

As was often the case, Henri knew without a word being spoken what Ramon was thinking. He shrugged. "I had to get Cinnia out of the house before they woke up and noticed she was gone. There wasn't time to shave."

Cinnia was a little more voluptuous than she had been before pregnancy, but it suited her. She rose on tiptoe to press her cheek to his and wrinkled her nose at his stubble. "He had a different shirt on. Then Rosalina spit up and he had to change."

"This is a setup, isn't it?" Isidora looked between the identical men, skeptical. "I mean, it was a safe bet that Henri might not have shaved, but..."

"I've seen it happen more times than I can count," Cinnia assured her, then picked up her husband's hand and said cheekily, "Be careful, Ramon. Henri wears a ring now."

Cinnia knew the engagement was a stunt. She didn't speak so loudly she risked exposing the ruse, but none of them laughed. Isidora blushed and dropped her gaze. Ramon felt a familiar clench of protectiveness, but it was directed toward someone different, which was such a new sensation it was disconcerting. Like the sensitive skin beneath a freshly removed cast.

"What—?" Cinnia began.

Henri tucked her under his arm and spoke over her. "I'll get the speeches done quickly. I want to dance with my wife while I have her to myself. Especially since we can't stay long." He squeezed her and drew her away.

Isidora's parents chose that moment to arrive, but the awkwardness only increased.

"My angel! We're so happy for you!" Francisca cried. "Have you set a date?"

"Hija preciosa," Isidora's father said as her mother moved along to fawn over Ramon.

"Papa." She leaned into her father's barrel chest to accept his enveloping hug.

"Estás bien?" He drew back to give her a searching look. Others had laughed at her puppy love for Ramon, but he never had. He didn't know about That Day, but he knew her reservations against taking this position at Sauveterre International had been motivated by a strong desire to avoid Ramon.

"I'm fine," she assured him. It felt like only a small lie. She was telling the truth in this moment, especially since she and Ramon had cleared the air in many ways, but she suspected that when this pretend engagement was over, she would not be "fine" by any stretch of the imagination.

Because he wouldn't marry her. That's why Cinnia's joke had landed so flatly, like a gob of mud on the bricks at their feet. She shook off the painful reminder and patted her father's lapel.

"How about you?" she asked with gentle concern. Every time her parents had reunited in the past, a painful breakup had soon followed, usually caused by her mother's tendency to wander.

Their experience was a cautionary tale, she reminded

herself, thinking of all the things Ramon had said that replaced her hurt and anger with wistful yearning and a blind desire to believe in miracles.

"Excelente," her father assured her with confidence.

Isidora wanted to believe him. As she watched them through the evening, staying close and sharing affectionate touches, she found herself hoping that this time they really would find happiness. But deep down, she knew she was just trying to believe in fairy-tale endings for her parents so she could buy in to one for herself.

Like her engagement dinner in the Paris restaurant, this evening was agonizing in its perfection. The moonlight turned the gentle foam on the sea to a veil of lace. The late summer breeze caressed like down. Henri and her father said warm things about how close their families had always been. Some of her dearest friends raised their glasses, genuine in their happiness for her, believing she was marrying the man of her long-held dreams.

When she looked up at Ramon, she almost believed it—which was so very dangerous, but how could she not be inexorably drawn to him? He was so confident, with features painted by a master into an archangel's, mouth curled in private amusement, body disciplined and still while his restless gaze moved across all he surveyed.

He was aloof and hard for a reason. Knowing those reasons only made caring for him more perilous. He wouldn't bend and nothing could break him. She knew better than to expect anything but heartache from him.

When they toasted with champagne, however, and the partygoers tapped their glasses, demanding a kiss from the happy couple, her heart raced with excitement. He took her in his arms and she knew that no matter what happened in the rest of her life, this man would always possess a piece of her heart.

She tensed slightly, as she had before all of his kisses, bracing herself to hide the way she reacted. She feared the blaze of need that flared when he touched her. It had only grown worse with proximity. This man had always had the ability to pull her outside herself and leave her standing without defenses, bare to the world. In the last few weeks, each and every time they had kissed, no matter how generic the peck, she had wanted to sob out at the pleasure-pain of it.

His embrace was too great a power to withstand, making her feel pried open.

But not being near him, not feeling his touch, *not* kissing him, was worse.

Until this moment, she had used fury and hurt to suppress all those feelings, but so much of her anger and agony was defused. She had little left to protect her. She was tingly and soft. Without conscious decision, she *yielded*.

He noticed. His gaze flashed as he slid his hand along the bare skin exposed by the cutout of her gown. He tucked his fingertips beneath the fabric as he drew her into him, the sheer propriety of his action making her heart stumble.

Other men had held her and kissed her, but no man except this one made the soft crash of their bodies feel like an implosion. All the energy was sucked from the surrounding area. It gathered tight inside her, releasing as a blast of excitement as his mouth claimed hers.

She really hadn't stopped thinking about their night. She tasted the memory on his lips, sipped again at the passion in the sweep of his tongue into her mouth. She hadn't stopped thinking about it, either, and abandoned chagrin in favor of welcoming the sensual storm he sent whirling through her blood.

In that moment, she knew he must possess *her*. It wasn't a clear-headed decision to make love with him tonight. It was a far more primal knowledge that whether it was tonight, or next week, or some point in the future, she would lie down with this man. Had to. Her mouth opened wider to accept his plundering kiss. Her body *yearned*. She wrapped her arms around his neck and stopped fearing he would destroy her.

She looked forward to it.

CHAPTER EIGHT

IF SHE HAD been a little bit drunk the last time she was in Ramon's arms, tonight she was high on natural chemistry. Pheromones. The imprint of a particular man's touch that never seemed to lift from her body even if it was only his eyes across a dance floor.

Not that he let other men monopolize her. No, he cut in shamelessly more than once, and reserved all the slow dances for himself. He said nothing, but he knew. He was too experienced not to.

She felt obvious and callow, but she was supposed to be a besotted fiancée, right? No one knew she was a virgin, though, least of all the man who would relieve her of that label.

They slipped away from their own party while it continued to rage, waiting until family was gone, then leaving the who's who to their follies.

With a signal, Ramon ensured the guards didn't let anyone else onto their elevator. The men stood at the front, giving her and Ramon the privacy of their turned backs.

Ramon didn't draw her into a hot embrace, though. He leaned his shoulder into the wall and gently drew her into the loose cage of his hands on her waist. His one hand moved against her skin within the cutout. His gaze went to where he traced that lazy pattern.

"I like this dress."

She choked out a laugh that sounded equally like a sob. The compliment was so bland. *Seduce me.*

His expression was solemn. He lifted one bent knuckle to stroke up her throat, then caressed beneath her chin, the action surprisingly tender.

The doors opened, startling her.

Ramon linked their fingers as they walked to their room and waited for it to be checked. Then he drew her inside and released her.

She stood for a moment in stasis, confused, aching, while he turned the lock behind her. Anxiety started to creep in at the edges of her consciousness. He was going to reject her. Again.

"Be sure, Isidora." The weight of his hands, solid and grounding, possessive, settled on her bare shoulders. For a moment, that's all it was, then he stepped closer, so she felt the graze of his tuxedo jacket, then the movement of his breath as he spoke against her hair. "I want to give you pleasure. I want that so badly you can't even imagine." His head rested briefly against hers. "But I don't want you to hate me after."

Because he wouldn't marry her.

She looked down at the clutch she held, then made herself move away from his touch to set the purse aside and face him. It wasn't easy. His focus on her was like a live wire, pulsing electricity through her in painful beats.

"I'm not a reckless person. I try not to do self-destructive things." She'd grown up watching it and knew better. She would proceed very carefully, she told herself. She wouldn't let herself get in too deep. "But I would always wonder."

She looked at where her hands tangled themselves together, not admitting the harder truth, that she feared she would never get over him until she had gone as far as she could with him.

"I know it would only be an affair." Her throat tightened, making the words rasp.

He flinched and the green of his eyes cooled to silver before he looked away. "You deserve better."

"I know I do."

That brought his attention back with a flash of reassessment that made her heart race into the base of her throat.

"I'm not a child, Ramon. Not anymore. You're right that you never could have met my expectations back then. But I do know what I'm worth and what I should expect from a man now, as a woman."

She turned the ring on her finger.

"I wouldn't normally go into something so intimate without at least the hope of long-term or permanent, but…" She sighed. "Maybe I am still a little naive, but I want to believe that even though this…arrangement is temporary, that we can be friends after."

A beat of silence before he made a jagged sound that wasn't quite a laugh.

"I left naive a long time ago, but I want to believe that, too."

"Then, yes. I'm sure." She held out her hands.

Ramon took her hands and pulled them behind his back, then his palm hooked the slenderness of her neck and he covered her mouth like he owned it.

And thrilled when she let him. She surrendered exactly as she had when he had kissed her downstairs. He had wanted to feast on her then and let himself do it now, kissing her hard, deep, taking and taking, allowing his hunger to consume him.

He wasn't a brute. He would have backed off if she had signaled he was moving too fast, but she worked her hands against his back, pulling herself tighter into him.

He caught fire under the friction, burning in a sudden conflagration that had only subsided since Monaco, waiting for the sough of her breath to burst into life again. He released her long enough to shed his jacket, dropping it to the floor, then growled like an animal as he caught her close and pressed her toward the bedroom.

The bed.

He was going too fast, he knew he was, but he'd never felt so greedy. So pressed for time. He wanted so *much*— the tendons in her neck, which made her gasp when he scraped his teeth there, the thrust of her mound against his aching erection, the fullness of her breasts weighing into his palms. Releasing her zip, he was able to draw down the one shoulder and find her braless, naked and firm, yet soft. So soft. And hot. Her skin scalded his hand as he cupped her breast, plumping it so her nipple sat high on the creamy swell. He bent to taste the hard bead, playing it against his tongue and loving her sob of pleasure.

Yes. Pleasure. He wanted to ask what she liked, how he could intensify this for her, but his voice was gone. He was barely able to form a thought beyond his desire to make her writhe and cry out and shudder the way she had in his lap.

Pressing her to sit on the bed, he climbed her gown up her thighs.

She gasped and her hand closed around his wrist.

"I only want to kiss you." He leaned to cover her mouth again, penetrated her lips with his tongue and groaned as she sucked on it. She shivered under the caress of his fingers over her breast. He let his touch linger there as he lowered to his knees between hers, kissing her and kissing her while he caressed and stroked and finally moved his hands to rub up the insides of her thighs.

When he found the silk between her legs and lightly stroked over it, she made a mewing sound, like music. He drew back to admire her swollen, parted lips, the dazed glow in her eyes, the way she bit her lip as he worked a finger behind the silk into heat. So much wet, slippery heat.

He pressed his finger into her honeyed channel, nearly out of his mind with how soft and ready she was.

She made a keening noise and her lashes fluttered. He stroked his thumb in a way that made her tighten all over, and she panted, "Oh, yes."

"Lie back," he commanded, feeling like a god when she sank onto the mattress and threw her arm over her eyes.

He worked black silk down her ivory thighs, taking his time unwrapping this gift. That's exactly what she was, with her thatch of red-gold and her nervous twitch as he slid his arms beneath the weight of her thighs. Pink and perfumed and heady. He wanted to make her scream.

Then he wanted to plunge into her and make her his. Indelibly.

Isidora was burning alive, driven crazy by the slide of Ramon's tongue, the way he pleasured her with his hand. Her fist knotted in his hair and she pinched her thighs against his ears, her abdomen twisting as an orgasm contracted in her. She lifted into his mouth, crying out, not caring how abandoned she was. It was too good, too fiercely good.

As her climax subsided, she lay there as a puddle of spent muscles and melted bones.

He rose over her, gaze avid as he studied her while roughly stripping his clothes.

She didn't move, only had a distant thought that her dress was the wrong color. It should be white. This was supposed to be a sanctified moment, not something raw and primal, where her thighs still burned with the scrape of his beard and he carried a condom in his pocket so he could roll it on without stepping away.

He pulled off her gown and pushed her higher on the bed as he covered her.

"My shoes."

"I like them." He guided her ankle to the small of his back, bit her earlobe and said something dirty about wanting to be inside her.

She had thought this moment would come on her wedding day, with declarations of love and a sweeter, more romantic deflowering.

But as imperfect as this was, lying atop a made bed, a man who would never promise forever pushing her legs apart, she couldn't deny she wanted this, too. She had never wanted anything so badly in her life.

He moved his tip against her slick folds, parting and teasing until she moaned, "Ramon," and lifted, offering herself.

He muttered something against her mouth and kissed her as he found her opening. He pressed in with a firm, deep thrust, pelvis coming up tight against hers as an inner burn seared and made her gasp.

He lifted his head, the haze from his eyes clearing. "Hurt?" He started to pull out.

"It's okay," she whispered hurriedly, trying to draw his head into the crook of her neck. Her heel instinctively pushed against his buttock, keeping him from retreating.

"Isidora," he breathed, eyes closing.

"Don't say anything stupid, Ramon. Don't—"

His eyes opened and realization was in them. Something golden and amazed that made the connection more than physical. Profound. It was like he saw inside her soul, glanced once, reached out and took possession of it. She had nothing left to shield herself. Everything she was had become his. It terrified her.

Something she couldn't decipher moved behind his eyes. He said something that was too soft and stark to catch. Dismay?

"Don't say you want to stop." Her voice was barely there.

"I am not that noble." He shifted, rocking their hips from side to side, settling deep again in a way that made her gasp. A little shudder went through her at the rush of sensations. Not pain, but acute sensitivity. Undeniable intimacy.

There was no pretending she was swept away. It was real. Indelible.

Yet strangely tender and sweet.

He propped on his arms, cupping the sides of her head in his hands. "This does change the tempo." He moved in a slow retreat and return, watching her. His eyes glittered, sharp and bright in the slanted light from the lamp. "I want to make it so good for you."

"You *like* that you're my first," she accused softly, biting her lip as a particularly sharp sensation glittered into delightful places.

"I do," he admitted, unabashed, dipping his head to suck her nipple, smiling with dark satisfaction when he provoked a wriggle and a gasp from her. He bent toward the other, and when she forced his head up, he added, "I like it more than I should. I can't wait to feel you come."

That sounded like he was impatient, but he took his

time, let her get used to the intrusion of a man while he caressed and kissed and complimented her.

It wasn't until she arched into him and said, "Ramon, I can't take this," that he laughed softly and moved with heavier, more wicked thrusts, giving her what she had unconsciously begged for. What she longed to keep each time he slid away, and welcomed with a noise of gratification each time he returned.

She didn't know what she thought sex would be, but she hadn't expected to flush all over, to want his teeth against her skin, his weight, his animalistic dominance over her.

It was base and elemental and made her moan and writhe and arch to offer herself until he pushed her into that glorious space where release burst over and around her, leaving her shivering and feeling like the most beautiful woman alive.

But she was alone again.

Still panting and dazed, she opened her eyes, betrayed yet again. "You didn't—"

"I will," he promised, shifting slightly so he could caress where they joined.

She sucked in a breath as fresh desire shot into her loins, making her clasp at his shaft. A latent pang of climax pulsed through her sex. She wouldn't have thought that could make her feel so turned on, but her limbs drew close around him of their own accord, trying to pull him more fully atop her, not even thinking, just knowing that she needed more of him.

"Tell me if I get too rough," he said as he loomed over her, voice gravelly and lips hot against hers. His kiss held nothing back and neither did his body as he pressed deep, quickly sucking her back into the whorl of mindless passion.

When he moved faster and harder this time, she wasn't sure she could take it. Not because it hurt, but because the intensity was so great, drawing her tight, threatening to cleave her in half. She needed this from him, though. Needed his unbridled desire, the possessive grasp of his hands on her shoulders. She wanted it. Gave herself up to it—to him.

And when the world exploded around her, she clung to his shuddering, damp form, listened to the echo of her cries in his hoarse shout and knew that once again, he had given her everything she had ever craved.

And still, it wasn't real.

CHAPTER NINE

FOREPLAY. AFTER-PLAY. SEX was play for him. At least it always had been.

Not with Isidora. Nothing in him felt light or humorous as he came back from the bathroom and found her naked, on her side, clutching a pillow to her chest. Her wary, sideways glance speared his throat, his gut.

He dragged down the blankets, shifted her feet, then the rest of her as he pulled her beneath the covers with him. He grabbed the pillow and sent it to the floor so nothing was between them but naked skin and silence.

After a second, she gave a shuddering sigh against his chest and relaxed in his arms. He relaxed at that point, too, oddly relieved.

"Did I hurt you?" There'd been a streak of red on the condom.

"A little. It's okay."

It wasn't. He didn't know how to react, but brushing off her virginity as trivial wasn't right. He knew that much.

"I wasn't, like, waiting for you or anything," she murmured. "Don't think I expect anything. There just hasn't been anyone I was that interested in doing it with."

"You let me believe you'd slept with Etienne."

She didn't say anything, only shifted her face against

his shoulder. He rolled onto his back so she could settle more comfortably against his side, and pulled her leg up so her thigh was across his waist, smooth and soft under his absent touch, twitching as he found a ticklish spot.

Should he tell her how closely he'd been watching Etienne, looking for an excuse to fire him?

"It was nice," she said so quietly he barely heard her. "Thank you."

"You're the Queen of Understatement, aren't you? It wasn't 'nice.'"

Her head came up and she looked appalled. "You didn't like it?"

She was a bright, confident woman, but still such an innocent.

"Of course I liked it," he grumbled, cuddling her into him again. "It was exquisite. *You* are exquisite." He wasn't a sensitive man. He knew how to charm, but rarely shared his true thoughts or feelings. Nevertheless, he admitted, "I will never forget it."

"Oh." He felt the word more than heard it. She swallowed and relaxed against him again. "That's sweet of you to say."

But she didn't believe him. Maybe that was for the best. He didn't want to lead her on, but it still bothered him. Their lovemaking had been incomparable. He'd been riding painted horses on a carousel all his life, then suddenly found himself atop a wild stallion. No, steering a purring race car. Flying a fighter jet. A rocket into space.

She wouldn't know how remarkable their connection was, though. Not until she moved on.

An uncharacteristic possessiveness struck him as he thought of her climbing into bed with other men, sharing her body, abandoning herself to passion, finding pleasure from *their* touch.

It was never going to be that good with anyone else. Did she realize that?

Was it fair for either of them to believe it?

He unconsciously tightened his arm around her, causing her to start, and she said, "Mmm?"

"Nothing. It's fine." He turned his lips against her hairline and inhaled her scent. He wanted her again. His body was hardening, longing to be inside her, but he reminded himself she was new to physical intimacy, so gently ordered, "Sleep."

Isidora had never slept with a man. They took up a lot of room. When she woke in the early hours, in a room so dark it was nearly black, she almost fell out of bed she was so close to the edge. She searched with a hand across the mattress for her pillow but found only warm, naked limbs. One snaked out to pull her tight against him. He was sinewy and hot, muscles flexing beneath satin skin. Hard.

"Where are you going?" he growled sleepily.

"Nowhere. I just…" She touched him. Couldn't help herself. She drew away enough to follow the line of silky hair down his tight stomach, then took his shape in her fist. He was smooth and ultrahot, his textures fascinating to her curious fingers.

He made a noise as she traced the arrowed ridge at his tip and pulsed under her touch.

"Did that hurt?"

"Hell, no. Don't stop."

She swallowed, surprised to feel a throb and rush of heat between her thighs. She was tender from their lovemaking, but in a way that made her feel secretive and luxurious and sensual. She stretched against him, wanting to feel him with every inch of her nude body. She thrust her nest of hair against his shaft and pressed him with her hand to firm the contact.

"I was trying to show some restraint, but if you're going to do that…" He kissed her and his hand stroked her thigh. He grew harder in her hand and shifted to suck her nipple, then asked, "Sore?" as he stroked into her wetness.

"No. It feels good." So good.

He rolled away and came back, then he was there, carefully pushing into her, thrusting lightly, then, when she moaned, with more power.

Somehow it kept getting better. The buildup was faster and more sure, the pinnacle higher, the release more complete. Maybe because he said, "Isidora!" like an incantation. The waves of pleasure expanded to her fingertips and toes, going on and on, both of them moving with it, playing out their mutual orgasm until they both settled to rest.

It happened again in full daylight, after they rose and showered. They fell onto the unmade bed for an energetic tussle that left them washed up like storm survivors, panting and damp, on their backs.

"This is insane. I can't keep my hands off you."

His words caused a pang under her heart. It was nice of him to say sexy things, but she expected he did the same for every woman he bedded. It was all part of his love-'em-and-leave-'em routine. Maybe he was even trying to make up for past hurts, wanting her to feel desirable.

She did, but she couldn't let the remarks mean anything beyond face value. Her father's eternal optimism where her mother was concerned was proof enough that some people were not a good risk.

Ignoring the slant of agony that pressed on her heart, she forced a wry tone and sat up, patting his thigh as she said, "You've been going without since our engagement. I wish I'd known sooner what I was missing. We're kind of experiencing a perfect storm. But now I need another shower. We really should get going or we'll be late for your mother's."

She paused as a thought occurred.

"I think we should, um, keep this on the down low." She waggled a finger between their naked bodies. "Do you mind? I don't want things to be weird with your sisters."

"Why would it be weird?" He curled his arm beneath his head, but she had the impression he wasn't nearly as relaxed as he looked. His glorious chest was tense despite their recent release, his gaze hooded by his spiky dark lashes.

Her hand lifted, wanting to pet him. He was so gorgeous, with his brown nipples on his toasted almond chest, his defined abdomen and his sex relaxed but still lengthened against his powerful thigh. She wanted to rise over him, straddle—

"What?" *Focus.* "I don't know. I just don't want them to think I'm still nursing a crush."

She would *die* if they teased her. It was bad enough that Trella had said last night that their kiss had looked "very convincing." Isidora had quipped something about practice making perfect, adding a roll of her eyes, pretending it was all a huge act. Trella had moved on to other things, but Angelique's gaze had lingered thoughtfully on her.

"Surely my privacy carries the same weight as yours?" Isidora said to Ramon.

Something flashed in his gaze, then he used a slow blink to hide his thoughts. "It does."

A stab of insecurity went into her belly anyway. She

didn't know why. Because this was new, she supposed. And it wouldn't last.

"Thank you," she said, lungs tight as she rose. She kept her back to him until she was putting on her face and able to keep her anxious thoughts hidden.

Ramon wasn't the sort of man who needed to keep his arm hooked around a woman, proclaiming to the world she was his. When he was in any sort of prolonged dalliance, however, like a week on his yacht, he enjoyed the affection that came between the bouts of sex. It was like petting a cat. The physical touches, the textures and warmth of her body, were as enjoyable for him as for her. He liked to keep them purring and content.

Isidora was right that they should keep things simple, but Sus Brazos was where he and his siblings came to unwind. It was the place they could be themselves without subterfuge or judgments.

And Isidora looked infinitely touchable with her hair loose—something she almost never seemed to do during the day. It tumbled in a mass of rich burgundy around shoulders bared by a sleeveless top in burnt orange. The color made her skin glow, especially where the collar was open down her breastbone.

He wanted to play with her hair and trace that narrow vee and draw circles with his palm on that firm ass of hers. She wore a pair of pants that looked like chamois, soft and buttery. They snugly cupped her figure and ended in narrow cuffs over sassy little boots that laced up like a spinster's, teasing him to find his lover behind the conservative facade.

Dios, he genuinely had to fight the urge to keep his hands to himself.

She forgot about him completely, enraptured by his

infant nieces. As she gathered Rosalina against her chest and buried her nose in the baby's neck, eyes closed blissfully, he caught a glimpse of what her future husband would see. His heart took a sharp corner, veering toward a cliff's edge. He had to look away.

And found Angelique watching him.

She was the intuitive one among them. A pulse of guilt went through him, like he'd been caught doing something he shouldn't.

He turned away from her and looked for Henri. He was speaking to Melodie, the family's official photographer, who was beginning to arrange everyone in front of the painting of their father.

Since the whole family happened to be here today, and Angelique was now married, their mother wanted a family portrait. It was a perfectly reasonable request, since Melodie had already been commissioned to snap Henri's new family.

Isidora came up to them and handed off Rosalina to Henri. "I want to check in with my mother," she said to Ramon. "She and Papa should be back in Madrid by now."

She slipped outside, but her weak excuse and even weaker smile stuck like a burr in Ramon's chest.

"Where did your fiancée go?" Melodie asked, stalling in surprise as she positioned Ramon.

"She's making some calls. Don't wait." He sounded peeved to his own ears, but this felt…inconsiderate. Isidora didn't belong in the portrait. She was never going to be part of this family in such an official way.

But he didn't have to rub her face in it.

Melodie blinked, astonished. "I see. Um, Trella, you stand here, then." She positioned Trella in front of him.

"He's engaged in image management, not marriage,"

Trella explained. "He's *helping* me." Glancing over her shoulder, she added, "Don't glare. You'll break the camera."

"If you're happy to tell the world that much, why not the rest?" He nodded at her prominent bump.

"Oh, please. Melodie isn't going to say anything to anyone."

"It doesn't change the fact you're being a hypocrite. Quit telling her my business and tell the father of your child he has one. Or let him off the hook if he's not. He's leaving messages with all of us, you know. *Return his calls.*"

"Did you just air *my* business in front of company? Now who's the hypocrite?"

"Faire taire," Henri growled. He was the last to move into position, along with Cinnia, and they each held an infant. "Do you know how hard it is to get two babies clean, fed and happy? Smile."

"Why do I even have to stand by him?" Trella growled, throwing an elbow into Ramon's diaphragm.

This was why he had always paired up with Gili. He glanced over at her, serene beside Kasim, glowing with joy. No doubt she would produce a new Sauveterre herself very soon.

He hadn't figured out how to handle this domesticity his siblings were embracing. It was far beyond what he imagined for himself. It wasn't a traumatic change, but it was still an enormous shift in his most comfortable dynamic. The foundation he depended on was rearranging itself.

Gili caught his eye and canted her head, expression concerned. Questioning.

He dropped his gaze. Trella's loosely curled hair cascaded down her back, too tempting to ignore. He reverted to when their lives had been simplest and gave one tendril a tug.

"He just pulled my hair!"

"Tattletale."

Everyone laughed. Melodie blinded them with a flash and said, "Perfect!"

A few more snaps—and snipes from his sister—and Ramon stepped away to nod at Henri. "*Así*. We need to talk."

Henri grimaced. "Rio. *Oui*."

It was their typical shorthand. They both knew that politically and financially, one of them should go to Rio for the commissioning of a port project Ramon had been overseeing for the last two years. The enterprise was Sauveterre's foundation in South America, establishing their expertise and credibility there.

"What are you talking about? Rio? You have to go." Sometimes they joked that if Trella had been old enough when their father had died, she would have pushed the two of them aside and taken over Sauveterre International herself. Maison des Jumeaux was the world's leading design house because she has a business degree in artist's clothing.

Certain things had held her back from reaching her potential, however, and Henri was as aware of them as Ramon. The trip had been planned before Cinnia delivered early and Gili had married and left Paris.

"You're not canceling. Not for me." Trella's jaw set.

Ramon ignored her, just held his brother's gaze. Their mother could step in if necessary, but she was better at helping Trella stay grounded. She wasn't as good with actual attacks, found them distressing and often fell apart herself.

"It's not that far if I have to fly back to Paris," Gili

said, setting her hand on her husband's arm. "Kasim understands."

"I'm right here," Trella interjected. "Telling you all that I don't want to be that person who needs hand-holding. How do I learn to cope on my own if you all keep rushing in? I *want* Ramon to *go*."

Ramon shook his head. He'd been down this road. "Bella—"

She spun to confront him. "If I want a man to be the boss of me, I will call the father of my child. You need to butt out."

"*Ça va,*" Henri said, holding up a hand. "Do not start World War Three. If something comes up, Gili and I will handle it. Go. Or you'll wake Colette and this will fall apart before Mama gets the rest of the pictures she wants."

Whatever Isidora had conjured in her innocent dreams as the perfect romantic honeymoon didn't come close to the reality of a week with Ramon in Rio de Janeiro. It was so much better and she knew that all future vacations with a man had been spoiled for her, along with all the rest of the things he'd ruined. Nothing would ever live up to this perfection.

The temperatures in South America were balmy, not hot, but the weather was glorious all the same. Not that the weather mattered. It could have been cyclone season and Isidora still would have been floating on a cloud of joy.

It didn't even bother her that they were working. They went into the company offices most days, at least for a few hours, then she ran to the site with him, smiled for photo ops, or stood by while he courted local officials at cocktail parties.

Ramon was as popular as ever with the paparazzi, having raced in São Paulo, but the animosity toward her was dying down so the attention felt quite friendly. She supposed people were beginning to believe it really was true love that had motivated him to quit racing. He certainly gave that impression, acting attentive, playing the part of enamored fiancé very convincingly when they were in public.

Heck, she was falling for it. She told herself it was nothing more than a revival of her old crush, this time more of a sexual infatuation, but she couldn't help feeling connected to him and he made it seem like it was reciprocated.

Because he wasn't putting on a show. At least, she didn't think he was. He was every bit as thoughtful and charming in private as he was for an audience. They retreated to his penthouse as often as they could, where he lavished her with attention. Whether they drank coffee in robes as they overlooked the ocean, or drank wine under the stars in his jet tub, his bare foot might seek hers, or he might pull her to sit with her back against his front. It was seduction, but at a slow pace. They made love constantly, but he was just as prone to maintaining physical contact afterward as before and during. He said sweet and sexy things, but they talked about other things, too. They debated world events and types of music and theater versus film. They bantered and rolled their eyes at each other and sent each other cheeky texts.

And then, when they had been scheduled to leave two days ago, he had said, "Why don't we stay and do the final coffee reception with the team. The view is something everyone should see if they've come all the way to Rio."

It had meant another night of lovemaking, another

day of feeling like a spoiled bride on her honeymoon because he wanted her to experience something he knew she would like.

Now she stood at the rail of Páo de Açúcar, Sugarloaf Mountain, and the view *was* amazing. She looked back on the cable car that had brought their team up. Wispy clouds decorated an intense blue sky, and far into the distance Rio de Janeiro sprawled in a river of concrete gray through the valleys between high, green-coated peaks. A lazy line of sandy beach drew a border between the land and the green-blue water that stretched endlessly into the horizon.

She felt as though she stood on the top of the world.

She loved him for extending their stay and bringing her up here. For wanting to spend more time with her. For making her feel like she was loved back.

She loved him.

Oh, no.

As she took in the dizzying view from what felt like the top of the world, fingers clinging to the rail, everything fell away below her. It was nothing but down, down, down.

Which was how far she had fallen for Ramon. Not a crush this time. The real thing. The most devastating kind of love. The all-in, heart-surrendered kind of love.

Oh, no.

Ramon's warm hand settled beneath her clipped hair, finding the crook of her shoulder at the back of her neck. "Good thinking—"

She knew immediately it was him, but was so deep in thought, instantly so fearful of him finding out, she reacted with a flinch and a startled gasp.

He gave her a little frown. "I only wanted to say it was good thinking to arrange this as a thank-you. They're all taking selfies and posting to social media, exactly the sort of excitement we want to convey. Are you all right? You're pale."

"Vertigo." She turned away from the view of paradise, stomach still plummeting into the abyss. "That was the idea when I suggested it," she murmured, feeling like that day he had proposed to her in front of the cameras was a million years ago. So much had changed, yet nothing had. "I didn't expect to be here enjoying it with them, though."

"I'm glad you are. Here, I brought you one."

Was he glad to be with her? Or had she been conjuring happiness all week, wanting to believe in a mirage?

She accepted the mug he held and watched him pick up one he'd set on the rail. She sipped, needing the rush of sugar and caffeine to help her get a grip on her composure.

"I don't know if I'll be able to go back to my French press after this."

"I only drink *cafezinho* when I'm here. It doesn't taste right anywhere else."

"Ah. Well, since this is our last day, and I probably won't be back, I'll have to appreciate this last taste, won't I?"

A beat of silence followed. She went over her words in her head, wondering if he heard the parallel. How much longer would she enjoy *him* and then never taste him again?

"I was thinking about extending our stay again. Would you like that?" He squinted into the view. A muscle pulsed in his jaw. "You haven't seen the statue."

Christ the Redeemer, he meant.

Her pulse skipped and she was windmilling her arms over the gorge again, anxious to latch on to what sounded like feelings of being equally enamored on his side.

"That's up to you, isn't it?" She stung as she said it. She had completely handed him the keys to their relationship. He steered it. He decided how far they went. Now she really did feel sick and heavy, the ground rushing up at her.

She opened her mouth, not sure what to say, how to recover, when an unusually loud jangle brought his hand to his chest pocket and a fierce, terrifying look to his face.

"What—?"

"That's the emergency ringtone." His hand slid to her upper arm and he drew her toward a quiet space away from the edge, where they had a semblance of privacy while he flicked through his phone.

His teeth bared. "Every. Damn. Time."

"What's wrong?"

"The prince of Elazar has Trella."

CHAPTER TEN

RAMON COULDN'T BELIEVE he'd let himself become so distracted. Lingering an extra two days was bad enough, but he'd been on the brink of adding to that shirking of responsibility. He was furious with himself.

In silence, he got them back to the penthouse, where they gathered their things for the flight he'd just moved up. They would take off the minute they could get themselves to the tarmac.

He packed light at the best of times and had been coming and going from this penthouse for twenty-four months. He was ready in minutes, but Isidora had managed to imprint herself all over the place. A pair of shoes here, a lipstick there.

As he moved around, picking up various items, he tried not to think of his participation in littering them about. He had pulled that hair clip from her tidy daytime chignon as she had shyly taken him in her mouth. That scarf on the end table had made a loose figure eight around his wrists as she straddled him and playfully took control for an erotic hour. He had even left a pair of her silk cheekies in the pocket of his suit, when she had let him bend her over his desk the other day at the office. They had fought groaning aloud so they wouldn't be heard and he had to bite back a mixture of frustration and renewed desire now.

This *had* to stop.

He found the scrap of lace in the jacket in the closet and threw everything he'd collected into the open suitcase.

"Thanks." Her mouth quirked and she blushed self-consciously, turning away to gather tubes and small color palettes off the dresser to put into a cosmetic bag. "Were you able to reach Trella?"

"No." Trella had given Henri her security code herself and seemed to be staying with the prince voluntarily, but she was having an attack, according to Gili.

Isidora glanced at him. "Is Angelique going to her?"

"No. And she shouldn't have to. She's the queen of Zhamair. *I'm* the one who should be on hand for that."

Isidora paused in pulling the drawstring on a shoe bag. Her lashes swept low across cheekbones that darkened with color.

"Am I being blamed for that?" She threw the bag into the suitcase and closed it.

"Not directly."

"Ah." She smiled flatly as she reached to zip the case. "I'm the enabler."

"I shouldn't have let my libido do my thinking. I know better."

She breathed out sharply, as if she'd taken a hit to the solar plexus. "Look, I know you're upset, but—"

"You *don't* know. This is why I will never have a woman in my life. This—" He motioned to the space between and around them, the crackling physical connection that had been so enthralling he had ignored the world outside it. "This ends now."

Her head went back, taking it on the chin with a flare of shock in her gray eyes.

He braced himself for an argument. Wheedling. Some kind of resistance.

She only offered a slow blink of acceptance, and somehow that was worse.

"Bueno," she said softly and turned to lift her case off the bed.

He was so shocked, he didn't move. He listened as she took it to the door herself, the rolling wheels loud across the ceramic tiles. When he finally moved to join her at the door, his joints felt stiff, words jammed sideways in his throat.

The silence wasn't an angry one, but it blistered as they traveled with their security detail to the airport and boarded his private plane.

He told himself not to dwell on whether he had stepped on her feelings. She understood. She had gone into this with her eyes open. His fixation on her was the root of his problem right now. He shouldn't have started their affair.

The flight was twelve hours. They both dozed in their seats rather than moving into the state room, as they'd done on the way over. No lovemaking this time.

As they touched down in Paris, Ramon arranged for Isidora to be taken to his apartment while he continued to Elazar alone. He didn't ask her if she minded. Her reaction was a quiet "Please call me if there's anything I can do."

There wasn't. He saw her off the plane, then carried on to see his sister, aware of the empty seat beside him. Isidora's presence had been strangely calming, he realized. She hadn't intruded overtly. She didn't pretend to understand the monsters in his emotional closet. No one except those as deeply affected by his past really understood that part of him, but Isidora had still been sincere in her concern. She had been a quiet light, keeping him from losing himself to the dark scenarios exploding in his mind.

Those grim thoughts threatened to overtake him as he arrived at the palace in Lirona, the capital of Elazar, where he had to wait thirty minutes for security clearance. It was another twenty before someone escorted him to a private suite, where his sister was curled on the end of a sofa, looking like hell.

Failure coalesced in a metallic taste on his tongue.

"Why are you here?"

That took him aback. He studied the ravages of a bad attack. Her cheeks were hollow beneath swollen eyelids. Her lips were chapped where she tended to lick and chew them as she waited out her symptoms. She wore a thick, man's cardigan over a pair of loose silk pants and ballet slippers. She always retained a cloak of insecurity and low body temperature after coming down from the worst of it. She hugged her arms tight across herself, seeming pale and slight despite the bump at her middle.

"What do you mean, 'why am I here'? I'm here to *get* you."

"I told you not to come."

"You told Henri and Gili not to come."

"Well, I didn't expect you to drop everything, did I? You were in South America, screwing your brains out with Izzy."

He balked at having his affair with Isidora described in such base terms, and was shocked enough by Trella knowing they had been sleeping together to ask "You talked to her? When?"

"I didn't. Gili said she thought something was going on between you two and you just fell for the oldest trick in the book. Seriously? How *could* you?"

He pinched the bridge of his nose. "I just traveled

twenty hours to come *save* you." That's why his wits were so dull. It had nothing to do with a strange, gnawing ache that kept marking the absence of that sliver of light he needed like fire needed air. "You don't get to make me into the bad guy here."

"No." She jabbed the air with a finger. "You keep saying you're doing me a favor with this engagement of yours, but if you want to sleep with Izzy, that's on you. Don't claim it's something you're doing to benefit *me*."

"Look, what happens between me and Isidora is our business. Why don't you tell me what's going on here?" He waved his hand at the elegant parlor. It was a very well-appointed prison tower.

"How many times do I have to say this? What's going on is my business, not yours. At least I'm not taking advantage of Xavier's feelings. I'm doing the opposite of nursing false expectations. What are you letting Isidora believe?"

"Stow it," he growled. "I don't answer to you."

"Oh, you do. For some crazy reason Isidora has decided she would die for us, which none of us deserve, and you think that gives you license to sleep with her and break her heart?"

"I'm not breaking her heart." His memory flashed with the look in her eye as they left Rio, the slam of emotion that she had hidden by turning her back on him. Again.

The pit of his stomach grew heavy. He had pushed her away because he felt guilty. He couldn't have her *and* be what his family needed. The push-pull had made him snap.

But she had known they weren't going to last forever. She hadn't invested her heart in him. Not again.

Had she?

"No, you broke it a long time ago," Trella accused.

"She never said how. She has never once said a word against you to me, because that's who she is, but I know you did something."

"That was a misunderstanding." He sliced the air with his hand, ashamed when he thought back on how he had treated her. "We sorted it out."

"Isidora is a *good person*. She's *kind*. You don't get to hurt my friend and say it's my fault. Quit leading her on. Quit—"

"Shut *up*, Bella."

"You shut up."

"No, *you* shut up—"

The door flew open. A man of about his own age strode in. His commanding air would have made him the crown prince of Elazar even if Ramon hadn't recognized his blond hair and red sash beneath a tailored business suit. Three guards entered behind him.

"Leave quietly or I'll have you removed."

Ramon snorted, hands on his hips, heart pumping hard enough with agitation to want to accept the rougher side of that ultimatum.

"Don't." Trella's weight landed against him and she looped her arms tightly around his middle, protective for once, not clinging with fear. "I was saying things he didn't want to hear. We almost never manage to speak in a civil tone, do we? It's not our way." She dug her chin into the place above his heart as she batted a sugar-sweet look up at him. "But we love each other dearly, under all the cussing and yelling. Don't we?"

Her wrinkle-nosed grin infuriated him, but the vestiges of an emotional storm still haunted her eyes. He wanted to hug her and yell at her to quit making his life difficult, same as always.

He looped his arm around her and squeezed gently,

mindful of his unborn niece or nephew. "Who would I fight with if I didn't have you? Gili? She cries."

"Henri? He lectures. I guess we agree on one thing." She gave him another hug, then drew back, expression solemn. "Sometimes I need you, Ramon. All those times you showed up when I called makes it possible for me to work through this on my own now. I know that you *will* come if I ask. That means everything." Her brow lowered to a dark, stern line. "But until I ask, you *have* to *butt out*."

He dropped his arm and held up his hands. *"Bueno."*

"And be nicer to Iz—"

"No." He held up a finger. "Butting out goes both ways. And you *will* introduce me to your host." Her keeper?

Ramon shared a perfectly civilized meal with his sister and Prince Xavier. He touched base with his family, texted Isidora, then slept off some of his jet lag in a room with an exalted past-occupant list that went back four hundred years. By the time he was leaving, Isidora still hadn't replied.

He probably deserved that, but it bothered him, especially when Trella said, "The palace is handling my PR from now on. Whatever stunts you pull with Izzy could do more damage than good. Tone it down."

He left in a state of discontent, ears ringing with the knowledge his primary reason for cornering Isidora into their fake engagement was gone.

He tried calling her twice more while he was in transit, but she declined to pick up.

Quit leading her on.

Had he been? He hadn't let himself examine too closely what they were doing, which wasn't unlike him.

He didn't deconstruct the good things in his life. He enjoyed them until they reached their natural end.

Enjoyed didn't come close to his state of mind while he'd been with Isidora, though. Yes, the sex was out-of-this-world, but there had been something enormously relaxing about being in a relationship recognized by outsiders as inviolate. The pretty birds of prey who'd circled all his life had kept their distance. The weight of boring small talk at parties was cut in half. She made him look better than he was and when they were alone, she was equally witty, stimulating his intellect, keeping him on his toes.

She had known it was temporary, he reminded himself. But his chest felt tight. Had he let things become too intimate? Had his drawing it out made it seem likely to become permanent?

Maybe it was better he had scorned her again.

Another searing pain went through him, resisting that truth. If he needed convincing, however, the sick feeling that had accosted him when Trella's alarm had gone off was it. He hated being so vulnerable. He didn't want to feel so worried for yet another human being.

It was stressful enough that she was refusing to answer his calls.

He checked her security report, but everything was listed as normal. Even the social-media reports had calmed down as his fans began fixating on when their wedding date would be announced and whether they would produce twins, as Henri had.

Ramon clicked off his phone and tucked it in the pocket over the ache of regret that hung in his chest.

Definitely better to end things before she began to wonder about wedding dates herself, he thought bleakly.

Since it was office hours when he arrived in Paris, he went to work, but only found Etienne at Isidora's desk.

"Where is she?" he asked, scanning the empty room, accosted by a weird premonition that grew worse as Etienne blinked in bewilderment.

"She didn't call you? Bernardo had a heart attack. She's gone to Madrid. I've been waiting to hear if he'll pull through—"

Ramon walked out, already speed-dialing his pilot.

"Why didn't you call me?" Ramon's voice came in with his footsteps, behind her, dragging her from a sea of worry to a boatload of pain. When his hand settled on her shoulder, she stiffened in defense, not able to cope with both sources of anguish at once.

His hand left her and in her periphery she saw it curl into a loose fist. He moved to stand closer to the bed, his expression tightening as he took in how her vibrant father was gray and still beneath his light sheet. His face was obscured by breathing equipment, his arm tied to an IV bag. The room was eerily quiet. Just that low sough of manufactured breath, the muted blip of equipment a lonely signal, proclaiming his heart still functioned. Barely.

"Was your mother with him? Where is she?" He glanced around.

She gave her father's limp fingers a reassuring squeeze, only able to reply with a faint shake of her head, not willing to go there. According to her father's house-keeper, who had been the one to call Isidora, Francisca had packed a few days ago. She wasn't at her own home. Isidora had tried to reach her without success, which suggested she was away. Far away. With someone else. On a yacht, beyond coverage, perhaps.

So much for this latest reconciliation.

Isidora wasn't ready to face any of it. She would have to wonder if her mother's fickle soul had caused her father's cardiac arrest and that created such a division of loyalty in her, she thought it might break her clean in half.

Focus on the positive.

"He made it through the surgery. They say that's a good sign." Her voice was desert-dry, thin and arid.

He transferred his attention to her, frown deepening as he studied her. "You look exhausted. Have you slept? Eaten? How long have you been here?"

She vaguely recalled a nurse giving her a canned protein drink while she waited for her father to come out of surgery. She had meant to finish it, but couldn't remember if she had taken more than a few sips.

"Can you please stop asking me questions? I was talking to Papa in my head. I want him to know that I love him. You can go, if you want. I'm just going to sit here."

Ouch.

He wasn't going anywhere, not that he wanted to be in a hospital again. It hadn't been very long since he'd sat vigil with his brother, waiting for news on Cinnia. It was the most helpless feeling in the world.

But he couldn't let her face it alone.

He did what little he could, checking with a nurse for a prognosis, which was at the grim wait-and-see stage. He shared the update with his siblings, who were all troubled by the news, then found a coffee station. He made a cup for Isidora, heavily sweetened and creamed.

"Gracias." She sipped and set it aside, all her focus on her father.

Time crawled for several hours, then suddenly her mother fluttered in.

"Ah, mi ángel! Lo siento mucho. I should have been here sooner. I didn't have my phone. How is he?" Her tearstained face contorted with fresh anguish as she looked at Bernardo. She burst into fresh tears, one hand on the bed rail, the other going around Isidora's waist as her daughter rose to stand beside her. She turned her face into Isidora's shoulder and cried without reserve for several minutes.

Silent tears slid out of Isidora's closed eyes, but even he could sense her mixed feelings, her distancing as her mother came up for air.

Francisca's expression grew even more stricken. "You're upset with me. Why?" Her gaze swung to Ramon with alarm. "Did you—?"

He jerked his head in swift denial. Now was *not* the time to reveal Isidora's parentage.

He braced himself for Isidora to catch on and demand to know what they were hiding, but she didn't even look at him.

"I'm upset that you left him, Mama." Isidora's voice was that heavy, anguished thing that wrung out his heart.

"No para un hombre. To a spa. I swear." She grasped at Isidora's arms. "We argued and I needed time—"

"No, Mama." Isidora tried to shrug off her mother's touch. "I don't want to be in the middle of it."

"There's nothing to be in the middle of! You have to believe me, *querida.*" Her mother gave her a little shake as she searched her daughter's expression, her own growing frantic. Fearful. "He asked me to marry him again. I said I would move in, but he insisted on marriage. Now he may die—"

"He won't," Isidora quickly said, shoulders caving as she reached for her mother. "He'll pull through. He has to."

Francisca looked like a lost child as Isidora comforted her, completely the wrong way around.

Ramon looked away, dismayed by all of it. Suspicious that Francisca had been with a man, but he wasn't about to throw accusations around a room like this.

Not long after, the doctor told them Bernardo's vitals had improved.

Ramon convinced Isidora to let him take her home to rest. She was so exhausted, she didn't have any fight left in her and fell asleep in the car. She woke when they arrived and said plaintively, "I thought we were going to *my* home."

"Your mother's?"

"My apartment. The one I bought when I requested a transfer. I sent all the things you removed from my place in Paris. I was going to start unpacking."

"That will have to wait." She was a wreck. "We're here now." In Salamanca, at the villa built by his mother's ancestors in the nineteenth century, not that that made an impression on her.

She moved like a zombie as she accompanied him up the front steps of the family mansion, barely looking around.

This home was one of the places few people except immediate family ever entered. He had lived here as a child, until Trella's kidnapping had prompted their father to create the heavily guarded compound, Sus Brazos, in southern Spain. Like all their homes, this one had been retrofitted and secured to the nth degree, but retained its exemplary architecture and original grandeur. Their father used to say it was more stairs than house, but it had tremendous charm, with its stained glass windows, ornate scrollwork and marble columns. The staff took care of him very well and seemed genuinely pleased to see him. He felt good to be home.

"I know you're tired," he said to Isidora. "But I called ahead. The soup is ready. You need to eat."

She sighed with resignation and let him guide her into the stately dining room, where she lowered onto the velvet-covered chair he held for her. She smiled weakly as their *cocido madrileño* arrived, fragrant enough to make his own stomach pang.

As they were left alone, and the only sound was the quiet clink of spoons against bowls, she said softly, "It's okay. I already know."

"Perdóname?" He paused with his spoon in midair.

"Mama told you when you were sharing secrets that night, I suppose?" The low light cast shadows over her hollow cheeks, making her look that much more haunted with her bruised eyes and cloak of anguish.

His mind went first to how blindly he had walked into Trella's trap. He liked to think he learned from his mistakes.

"You'll have to be more specific. I'm not sure what you're talking about."

The corners of her mouth trembled as though she tried for a cynical smile, but didn't have the strength. He suspected there was disappointment there, too. In him, for making her spell it out.

"My mother has never had it in her to be exclusive to anyone. She cheated on my father a lot, right from the beginning. He married her because she was pregnant. He thought it would get better, but it didn't. He blamed himself. He traveled so much, working for your father." She waved her spoon toward him. "I don't say that to imply your father is responsible for her infidelity. Papa has no regrets about working so closely with him. When Trella was taken… He had a daughter. He wanted desperately to help, not be one of the vipers who tried to capitalize."

"We know." The words seemed to vibrate in the still, empty cavern that his chest became. "Bernardo was one of the few to take our side after our father passed, supporting us against the board. He has always been highly valued by our family. We're all upset he's in hospital."

"I know." She dropped her gaze to her bowl as she stirred her soup. "And he was an ambitious man when he was younger. He wanted to work that hard. When he did come home, he wanted that home to include his daughter, so he didn't confront Mama about her infidelity. He didn't want to divorce her. He knew she had been molded into what she was by her childhood. He didn't want a replay of custody battles and risk turning me into the same thing. But by the time I was starting school, he couldn't ignore any longer that I looked nothing like him."

Ramon set down his spoon and sat back.

"He knew she must at least suspect I wasn't his. He had a DNA test done and knew for sure."

"But he didn't confront her."

She shook her head. "He was angry enough to divorce her outright, but…he loved me." She smiled through a sheen of tears. "He knew he would lose me in a custody battle. I wasn't his. He didn't know what to do. He asked your father for advice and your father asked him, 'Who will be her father if not you?' So he stayed a little longer."

Her smile wobbled and turned down.

"I owe your father for that," she said huskily. "It wasn't easy for Papa."

He watched her swirl her soup, eating nothing, thinking of Trella saying "For some crazy reason she has decided she would die for us."

"This is why you agreed to our engagement." He

wanted to be alone then, to deal with the roaring, howling shame in him. Somewhere, in his past, his father had done something so noble and kind for this girl, it filled him with a swell of pride. His father had ensured Isidora had something she desperately needed, that she deserved, and he, Ramon, had come along years later, grabbed it roughly and used it without remorse.

"I love him so much." Her voice cracked. "I knew Mama was…not like other mothers. I used to lie to him about the men in the house, about where she had been. I lied to people all over the city, trying to cover up for her. I was so afraid he would find out and leave us. Leave me." She bit her lips together to still their tremble.

He drew a measured breath into lungs that burned.

"When your father died…" Her lashes came up and sent empathy to him that compressed his chest even further. "It hit Papa hard. He reassessed his own life, the sacrifices he was making in staying married. I think he thought if he divorced my mother, he would stop loving her, but that never happened. He told me everything once they started their proceedings, in case it came up. He didn't want me to be blindsided by it."

"But if you all knew at that point, why didn't you take it up with Francisca?"

She shook her head in a hopeless little gesture.

"Mama doesn't process relationships the way other people do. She didn't have parents who loved her so she doesn't know how to be a parent, doesn't understand how love works. That's why I needed Papa so badly. If I could have, I would have gone to live with him after they divorced. It was so disruptive to live with her. But if she had known that I knew he wasn't my father yet preferred him over her…? It would have killed her. I mean that almost literally. She's a broken person. She's desperate to feel loved and counts on me to love her no matter what. It's something that keeps her from completely self-destructing. To take that away from her, and reveal that I know she did this awful thing to my father… And what is the next step? Ask her about my biological father? Make her admit she doesn't *know*? She would expect that I would never forgive her. Maybe I wouldn't. I would lose her, that's for sure. One way or another she would disappear from my life. I can't risk that."

The slant of her shoulders, so heavily weighted, made his own ache. He carried a lot of pain himself, but in that moment, he took in the scope of hers and he was humbled.

"I'm really tired. Can I go to bed now?" She set aside her spoon.

He gave her barely dented soup a dismayed glance. "I'll take you up."

He put her in his own bed, watching her move like a robot on autopilot as she stripped her pants, then pulled her bra straps down her arms before digging under her shirt and throwing her bra to the floor. She was asleep before her head hit the pillow.

He watched her for a long time, wondering what would happen to her if *she* lost the one person she counted on to love her.

It had all been a bad dream. They were still in Rio and she had dreamed that he had ended things so ruthlessly. He hadn't dumped her in Paris like soiled laundry. She hadn't received a call that had shaken her to her very foundation.

Part of her knew that she was kidding herself, that she was in his bed in Madrid, but as her hands skimmed over the warm satin that was Ramon's hard body next to hers, she let herself travel back in time a mere few days, to when she had believed their future was bright and endless.

He responded by gathering her into his heat, murmuring something about her needing sleep.

"I am sleeping," she whispered against his neck, nuzzling the stubble under his chin with her nose. Her hand found his length, slowly worked up and down as he grew under her touch. "I'm dreaming. Don't wake me."

He said something she didn't catch, an imprecation, and dug his hand into her hair, pulling her closer as he searched for her mouth with his own. His heavy body rolled, tucking her beneath him.

Time slowed. He drew out each kiss, each caress, peeling open one button at a time down her shirt, then parting it to spread kisses across her chest. When he finally found her nipple, she was practically weeping, all of her skin sensitized, all of her being expanding with love for him.

"Touch me," she begged, pushing his hand between her thighs, where she was wet and aching.

He growled with appreciation, then stroked his hand on her inner thigh, spreading her legs wider to accommodate him as he settled between them. When he climbed his fingertips back to where she yearned, she gasped into his mouth.

He slid away, down and down, mouth following a leisurely path through the valley of her breasts while his hands cruised in tender caresses across her skin. His lips grazed the ridges of her ribs, played into the trembling plane of her belly, and finally his hot breath fogged the humid grove between her thighs.

He pleasured her, driving her up and up the rise of tension.

She stroked her fingers through his hair, blatant in

how she offered herself to him, joyous in her abandonment. No man would ever give her this again. She had to take it now. *Now.*

She cried out as a climax rocked through her, anguished that it was over so quickly, but he rose over her, moving away briefly for a condom, then settled on her again. As he slid into her, she sighed with repletion. All of her folded around him, drawing him in deeper.

He made love to her like that for a long time, slow and easy, as if he, too, wanted to prolong this connection. As if he knew, as she did, that this was their last time.

But it couldn't last forever and their bodies were too responsive to each other's. The friction of his movement was building to a screaming pitch inside her. She was so mindless in her arousal, her hands moved in uneven patterns across his shoulders and back. They slid of their own accord to his flexing buttocks and urged him to thrust harder. Deeper.

He pushed his hands beneath her buttocks and took her with him, driving ruthlessly. She closed her legs across his back and lifted herself into him, glorying in the animalistic act, thrilling to the roughness of it. The implacable imprinting of his body into hers.

On and on she clung to him, everything obliterated from her mind except him. This. Them. Timeless. Forever.

Then, suddenly, the world exploded. They both released jagged noises as a powerful climax overcame them both in a rush of culmination and abject loss.

CHAPTER ELEVEN

Isidora felt like an exposed nerve as they arrived at the hospital. She and Ramon hadn't spoken much, just exchanged the mundane things. Breakfast was ready. What time should he order the car, that kind of thing. She had showered alone, which had made her feel bereft.

Neither acknowledged their lovemaking, which had made her feel like it was something shameful that needed to be hidden, at least from herself.

She felt like her father, going back to her mother again and again, hoping for a better result. She had judged Bernardo at times, thinking him foolishly optimistic and a glutton for punishment. Now she judged herself the same way.

At least they would have a clean break.

Her father was awake when they arrived, still very weak, but the doctor was there and pleased with how things were progressing. He was recommending a move out of intensive care and discussed the plan for his recovery at home when he was discharged in a week or two.

"I'll stay with him," Isidora said, smiling through her relieved tears at her father, not looking at Ramon as she said it. He couldn't argue. It was a perfectly legitimate reason to end their pretend engagement.

"Oh, no, *querida*," her mother protested. "You have

a wedding to plan. So do I." She smiled, glowing as she gazed at Bernardo. "Of course I'll be your father's nurse. In sickness and health, *correcto, mi amor?*"

"But you said—?" From the way her mother had spoken yesterday, she had thought Francisca didn't want to marry again.

"I told you, that's why I went away. I needed to think. To be sure, but yes. Almost losing my one true love has convinced me." She leaned to kiss Bernardo's waxen forehead. "Of course I will marry you, *mi amor.*"

Her father's breathing tube was gone and his white lips managed a small, cherishing smile.

"Papa—" She stopped herself, unable to protest their trying again. Her mother would take it as a lack of support.

She didn't know where to look as she fought letting all her bitter, angry, confused, angst-ridden thoughts fly out of her tight throat.

Ramon moved in close behind her and rubbed his hands on her upper arms.

"Congratulations," he murmured over her shoulder to Bernardo. "We're both very happy for you. Francisca, did you spend the night here? You must be exhausted. Let me order a car, so you can go home for some rest. We're in no hurry to get back to Paris. Isidora will want to sit here awhile and assure herself Bernardo is on his way back to fighting form." He walked her mother out.

Once they were alone, Isidora met her father's eyes. Her brimming eyes overflowed in a pair of tracks down her cheeks.

"Papa... She *left.*" Her hands locked around the bed rail, blurred eyes taking in the equipment that had kept him alive when his heart had given out. Did he not see that this time her mother had, in actual fact, *broken* his heart?

"I love her," he whispered. "I have to give us another chance."

No, he didn't.

But he would.

"What are you going to do?" he asked, gaze sliding to the door where Ramon had disappeared with her mother.

She shook her head. She couldn't move back here and watch her parents struggle and implode again, but she couldn't continue with her farce of an engagement, not when she saw what a physical toll misguided love could take.

She refused to keep giving chances to someone who would never love her back.

Isidora was introspective all the way back to Paris. Ramon couldn't blame her. He was a private man himself, especially when a family crisis occupied his thoughts, but he found himself wanting to draw her out. Reassure her.

"Are you upset about your parents reuniting?" he asked as he poured them glasses of wine.

"Hmm?" She seemed to come back from a long way away. "Oh. Worried, I guess. I learned a long time ago that their relationship is not something I can control, though."

She took the glass he brought her with a murmur of surprise. *"Gracias."* She returned to her pensive study of the closed drapes. She wasn't being cold, just quiet, which seemed worse.

"Do you want to watch a movie or something?"

"No," she murmured, that absent voice entirely too lethal. "I'm going to pack."

He heard the words, knew what they meant, had even expected them on a subconscious level, but he wasn't prepared for them. He wasn't prepared for the way the handful of short words set him into a barren arctic waste-land, where snow blew in a fuzz of white, making him feel blind and deaf. Abandoned.

"I don't expect to sleep together," he said, then realized how stupid it sounded.

Her head came around and her lashes came up, revealing the gray of her eyes to be a bleak mist. Her mouth curled into a mockery of a smile, but the least amused kind. He half expected her to say she hadn't invited him to.

"I know."

What did she know? He didn't know anything. His brain was as empty as his soul. Something in him leaped to thinking he could survive without sex. He would hate it and burn with need, but he could live without holding her as long as she stayed in his life.

"You can't—" He cut himself off, unable to find the reason she couldn't leave. His sisters had moved on to new, very safe situations. His brother would handle the sensation caused by his own children. Even the online trolls targeting Isidora had subsided to something to keep an eye on, not truly fear.

"I can't play pretend anymore." Her voice held only a small rasp, but it was as gritty as sandpaper across his ears, making every hair on his body stand up. "And it's never going to be real. Is it?"

It wasn't a question. She was confirming a fact. Her parents' relationship was not something she could control and neither was he.

The way she looked at him so nakedly, heart open so he could see how desolate she was in her acceptance of this hard fact, pushed him into the maw of a black hole.

"No," he agreed. Had to. The kindest thing he could do for her was free her of him once and for all.

Still, the way her breath caught in a hiss made him feel cruel. He wanted to apologize, but she nodded distantly and turned away.

She didn't see his hand lift, clench into a fist and get forcibly pushed into his pocket.

She disappeared into thin air.

She went from his apartment to the secure flat above Maison des Jumeaux. He knew that much, but a week later, he realized she had slipped out of Paris and he had no way to trace her. She took over paying her security team and that was that.

It threatened to drive him mad.

Ramon knew this feeling. He hated it above all others. It was precisely the reason he was so careful about allowing people into his heart. Worry gave him a vulnerability, a pressure point. It was a type of gnawing pain that never ceased.

He barely slept, either spending the night conjuring a kind of hell he didn't want to contemplate, or recalling the heaven he'd had. He woke in an empty bed and checked his phone, saw no messages from her and was forced to wonder where the hell she was. With whom.

Her father said she had taken a PR position with a very exclusive client. He didn't know who it was, but she had assured him she was happy and well looked after.

After another two weeks, Ramon broke down and called Killian, their security specialist. "I want you to locate Isidora for me."

After a beat of surprise, Killian admitted with a hint of reluctance, "I can't fulfill that request."

"Why the hell not?" Then, with suspicion, he asked "Is she working for you?"

"No."

"A client?"

"You know I don't discuss clients."

"I love this conversation we're not having, Killian. Can you give me proof of life? Is she well?"

"Yes."

It was a relief, but a very small one. Killian wouldn't say where she was or how he knew. He had clients all over the world so Ramon had to continue to speculate.

When Angelique called a few days later, claiming to be homesick, and begged him to visit, he complied. She was always comforting to be around when he was unsettled, but the minute he landed, he was uneasy, wanting to be in Paris in case Isidora turned up there, looking for him.

Why the hell would she look for him? He had savaged her heart yet again.

"I was surprised you agreed to come," Gili said as he was shown into her obscenely lavish private apartment inside the palace of Zhamair. "When we were here for Sadiq and Hasna's wedding, you were quite put out at the cultural restrictions, if I recall."

Her gentle teasing came with a hug that contained volumes of an embroidered dress with a cape. Her head was loosely covered in a beaded scarf, her forehead graced with chains of gold. Her eyes were made up with dramatic dark liner and thick lashes, but this was no stranger. His compassionate sister lurked in her searching gaze as they drew apart.

"Chatting up women doesn't interest me the way it used to," he admitted grimly, making a restless turn past an ottoman to a tinted window that overlooked the well-watered grounds. "Have you spoken to her?"

"Who?"

He sent her an impatient look. "Isidora. Trella said

you suspected more was going on with our pretend engagement. Has she been in touch? Said anything about where she is? What she's doing?"

Gili adjusted the fold of her scarf alongside her face. "When she called to ask to use the Paris flat, she said things didn't work out between you, but she has always drawn a line between our friendship and her feelings for you." She moved to sit and carefully arranged her skirt. "She has never once tried to prevail on us the way other women have, to try to get near you and Henri. That's why we love her."

Love. He shoved his hands in his pockets, fearful that that was the root cause of his discontent. He used to like using Gili as a sounding board, but suddenly he was loath to open up. The things he had shared with Isidora, the way she made him feel, were far too personal to reveal to even his most trusted sibling.

"It's why I wanted to help her when you broke her heart yet again," she murmured.

He whirled around. "You— What do you mean? You sent her somewhere?" His brain clicked to the answer very quickly. It made perfect sense, but he still couldn't believe it. "She's *here*? Working for *you*?" The sense of betrayal was startlingly sharp. "Why would you keep that from me? Does Henri know? Does Trella?" His tone was a lot harsher than he would normally take with her.

Rather than tear up, however, his sister folded her hands in her lap and set her chin, regal in the way she regarded him. Angelique was always toughest when defending those she loved and right now, he knew exactly whose side she was on. Not *his*.

"She deserves a chance to heal in private, after you made such a spectacle of her."

He grimaced and looked away.

"But when Killian said you were concerned about her, I thought I should let you know that she's perfectly safe. She has a room here in the palace and forms part of my entourage when I have royal duties. We're all under royal guard. She's safer here than she would be anywhere," she mused. Then she grinned like her old self as she confided, "I almost miss the tourists and the selfies. The press is so respectful here, it's kind of funny."

He was glad for her and wanted to hear more about that, but not right this second. "I want to see her."

She sobered. "Why? Just because she hasn't given me details doesn't mean I can't see how miserable she is. If I thought you loved her—"

"I *do*." It came out through clenched teeth—he'd resisted to the very last second. It came with a wrench that reframed his heart, cracking the vault, spinning the dials, opening to allow her in, then sitting agape. That aching sense of exposure was nearly more than he could stand. "Take me to her, Gili. *Now*."

Isidora was living a fairy tale, the kind that took place over a thousand and one nights.

Her job was much the same work she'd been doing for all the Sauveterres, but she focused on Angelique now. Kasim had a team that handled his palace concerns, but she had been hired to comb the English-language sites, addressing rumors that specifically affected his wife, especially anything that had the potential to reflect poorly on her, his country, or his ability to rule.

From a career standpoint, the job outshone even the Sauveterre name on her CV. On a more personal level, while her boss was a man, she rarely needed to speak directly to him. She had two female coworkers and, since fraternization between the sexes was discouraged, rarely spoke to any men at all.

She was making new friends and helped keep Gili from feeling homesick. They lunched together a few times a week, practiced their Arabic on each other, visited the spa together and traded opinions on the designs Angelique's team sent from Paris. Sometimes, if Kasim was tied up for an evening, they ordered a Western movie and watched it in Angelique's private chamber.

Isidora thought her own lodging plenty fit for royalty. It was ridiculously beautiful for a midmanagement PR clerk, not that she would dare to say so and risk being kicked out of it. More of a bachelor suite, the sleeping area was part of the main room, but the space was enormous. It had marble floors, a lounge and dining area, and a pretty screen to hide the dressing area that also led to an attached bathroom.

It was like living in a hotel. She ordered food by speaking to her personal attendant and her meal was delivered hot and fresh at the requested hour. Tonight she said, "I'll call you when I've finished my swim."

Her private bathing pool was too tiny for laps. She could walk end to end in its waist-deep, kidney shape in less than ten steps. It sat under a trellis in a walled garden, where a handful of birds sang and fluttered amid a riot of colorful blooms from climbing roses to dangling fuchsias. The fragrances off the lavender and lemongrass, cloves and saffron, were exotic and dream-inducing—it was the perfect place to relax.

She poured herself a glass of cordial, stripped naked next to the pool and waded down the steps. As the water lapped at her knees, then her thighs, she sat—as she did every evening—and let the agony she ignored all day overtake her.

Because this beautiful life did not make her happy. She missed Ramon. So badly. The tears coming out of her eyes were drawn directly from her heart, squeezed out with each clenched beat.

With her elbows sitting in the water, braced on her submerged thighs, she let her tears run through her fingertips, certain she was what filled this pool every day, not the underground spring her attendant claimed.

And when she heard a footstep, and flung up her head, mortified to have her attendant catch her like this, she was even more appalled to see a man. *The* man who had reduced her to this.

She cupped some water, splashed her face to clear her eyes and, yes, Ramon still stood there in a pair of his scrupulously tailored pants. His crisp button shirt was open at the throat and strained across his chest as he set his hands on his hips.

She couldn't meet his eyes. She ducked her head, crossed her arms across her front and drew her feet up a step. "What are you doing here?"

"Visiting my sister," he said flatly.

"Wrong room."

"I've been worried about you."

"I don't want to talk to you, Ramon. Not like this. Let me get dressed."

In her line of vision, she saw him toe off his shoes, then his pants skimmed down and landed in a ball of charcoal, quickly topped by navy colored shorts and a pair of black socks.

She clenched her eyes shut, not watching the rest. "What are you *doing*?"

"You sounded uncomfortable that you were naked and I was clothed." The water rippled and he sighed. "This is nice."

"You are *such* an impossible man." She hid her face behind her hands, huddling to protect her nudity, still feeling teary, but for an entirely different reason. Some horribly sick part of her wanted to hope, but it was so futile. "They have pools elsewhere, you know. With your connections, I'm sure you could get your own right here in the palace."

"I spoke to your father. He sounds well."

Her parents were muddling along, waiting until her father was fully recovered to plan their wedding. They weren't yet falling apart, but it was early days. She wouldn't get her hopes up any more than she would with Ramon. Why was he here?

"Isidora. Look at me."

"No."

"Why not?"

"Because you'll talk me in to whatever stupid thing you want me to do and I refuse, okay? You have come to the well once too often."

The water swished and she mentally pictured his strapping form gliding toward her. Her pulse tripped. Water swayed against her, licking sensually, teasing her into wanting to open her eyes.

"Ask me why I spoke to your father." His voice was at the far end of the pool.

"No."

"No matter what I ask of you, you're going to say no? Is that what I'm hearing?"

"That sounds like a trick question. I refuse to answer."

"The trouble with an intelligent woman," he muttered.

"Better than being a stupid one."

"Do you feel stupid for loving me?"

Present tense, like he knew how deeply she had fallen for him. Fresh tears pressed the backs of her aching eyes.

"No." She finally lifted her head and opened her eyes.

He had his arms outstretched against the pool's edge, shoulders gleaming, hair wet, cheeks stubbled and rugged. The desert sky was fading to mauve and the pin-prick strings of white lights that wound through the trees were coming on.

It was magic, pure magic.

Not real.

A line of fire stretched from the back of her throat to spread burning fingers around the walls of her heart. "But I would be stupid to let you take advantage of my love again. I won't, Ramon."

"I want you to marry me, Isidora."

"That's—" Cruel. "Why? What happened? Never mind. I don't want to know. *No*, Ramon." She started to rise.

He pushed off from the end, striking through the water like a crocodile, barely giving her time to react beyond pressing backward into the hard edge of the step behind her before he was right there, eye-to-eye, arms caging her, water sluicing a pattern down his chest hair between them.

"Why not?"

"Because I won't go through that again." She put up a hand to ward him off, but he eased onto one elbow, then another, so he bracketed her very tightly, practically nose-to-nose.

"We're good together."

"Sexually? You can get that anywhere."

He sizzled with temper as he pierced her with a hot, green stare. "No. I can't. It's different when you love someone."

Her heart flipped and tumbled, creating such a jumble of emotions in her that she pressed his shoulder, silently begging for space to assess and understand. To keep her head so she wouldn't follow her foolish heart into believing the impossible.

"Don't—don't say that. You don't even know me. You don't—"

"I *know* you." So askance.

"You know what I like in bed." She couldn't say it without her stupid voice creaking and, yes, she was starkly aware they were naked. Why the heck was he doing this to her like this, keeping her off-kilter and completely defenseless? She was half seduced by his nearness alone and refused to look down, even though she was quite sure she knew what that firm shape was that was nudging her thigh.

"You—" She cleared her throat and kept her hand firmly on his shoulder, holding him off. "You know that you can talk me in to anything. You don't want a wife. You want a PA who puts out."

His expression edged toward thunderous. "Is this you demonstrating how well you know me? Because I'm beginning to doubt *your* love."

She narrowed her eyes. *Her* love had been born so long ago, it was celebrating double-digit birthdays.

The corners of his mouth curled, which almost scored another hit, but then he said gently, "That won't do, will it? The absolute worst thing I could do to you is underestimate how much you care for me, isn't it? You see? I do know you."

He moved backward, but somehow he gathered her off the step and pulled her with him. She instinctively clung, expecting to sink, but his hard, warm body kept her afloat.

"I know that when you eat, you start with the vegetables. You eat as much of what's good for you as you think you have to, then switch to what you really want before you get too full and abandon what's left. You're always trying to find the balance between what you think you *should* do against not cheating yourself. Which is why you became my lover. It's also why you walked away when the cost became too high."

She wriggled, trying to find her feet, but he was in control, tapping a side wall so they gently rotated back to the steps. A moment later, he settled on a stair low enough to submerge them to their shoulders, and gathered her into his lap.

She kept herself sitting up straight, perched on his thighs, trying to ignore the light play of his fingertips against her hip.

"It's why you're holding me off right now, even though I would bet my fortune that you are as physically ready to make love as I am." A slight shift let her drift in to feel his hard flesh against her buttock.

She gasped and tried to angle herself away.

Even though he was hideously correct. A secretive throb was pulsing between her thighs and she had to fight the urge to let her arms twine around him, to let their lips meet and their bodies rub, and deal with the reality of such foolishness in the morning.

His expression sobered. "I also know you have a capacity for forgiveness that scares me, because I know you're going to be hurt—by me, by your parents, by some other person who I'll want to kill for treating you carelessly... I can't prevent it, though, because you lead with your heart. You'll always put yourself out there, trying to save the world one bolstering hug at a time. Emotional pain doesn't scare you. Hurting people, letting them down, scares you. Why is that?"

She looked down, shocked by that. Profoundly shaken.

"Was it because your mother was so easily hurt? Because you saw how traumatized Trella was? How broken we all were, and you had to do what you could? That sounds like you, doesn't it?" His thumb kept up that lazy pattern against her upper thigh. "Generous. So easy to love."

"Ramon," she protested weakly, closing her eyes to hold the burn inside her lids.

"Why else would I have gone to such lengths to push you away? Hmm? I was half in love with you, scared to death. I didn't *want* to love you. No, don't let that hurt. Listen."

He pulled her close even as her face contorted and she tried to press away, trying to turn from the anguish.

"Listen to me," he said, mouth against her temple, arms strong around her cringing body, holding her together as the seismic shifts he was sending through her threatened to crumble her apart. "I didn't want to add to my list of people to worry about and fear for. I didn't want to put a woman at risk by giving her my name. How could I ask anyone to make children with me so we could fear for them? All of that scares the hell out of me, Isidora. *But my love for you is bigger than that.*"

She drew back, mouth pulling at the corners so she had to bite her lips to still their tremble.

"It's true," he said gently, beautiful face open and grave. "I can even tell you the day when my feelings began to overtake my fear. When you refused to dance with me at your father's birthday, I realized that I might have lost you. You weren't dead, but I was. To you. I told myself it was for the best, that I didn't care." He traced a wet thumb along her jawline. "But I cared. I felt dead."

She tucked her chin, sheepish. "I was pretty mad. I really did want to get over you."

"I know you did." He was very, very solemn. "And when Henri hired you, I was so grimly pleased you were being forced back into my life without my having to chase you."

"You never chase women."

"No, I don't. But I've been hunting for *you*. I thought I knew how badly I would miss you, but it's been a living hell, Isidora."

She made a scoffing noise and let her body melt into his, seduced by his words, one arm going up to his neck. "You miss the hero worship."

"Is that what that abuse was during our engagement?" His mouth quirked as he nuzzled his nose against her chin. "I happen to love that you aren't afraid to take me down a peg. I'm not an easy man. Living with our kind of attention and security can be a nightmare. You have to be tough to withstand it and the fact you can find a smile in all of that, and make me smile...I'm the one in awe of you, Isidora."

She balanced on a razor's edge, but this time she knew she would fall. One side was hope, the other belief.

"Is this real, Ramon? Because if—"

"It's real, Isidora. Ask me why I spoke to your father."

"To ask him where I was?"

"To ask his permission to marry you."

"Did you really?" She teared up, incredibly moved. "He must have been so touched. Thank you for that."

She gave in to desire and slid from her balance on his thigh, using the buoyancy of the water to inveigle between his legs, so they were chest-to-chest, her knees bumping between his flatly planted feet.

She would have kissed him, but he drew back a little. "Is that a yes?"

"To marriage? Kiss me and I'll think about it."

"Not good enough, *mi amor*. I want—"

"I know what you want." She used her arms around his neck to draw herself up and down his length, pleased when his breath hissed in and his hands tightened on her.

In a sudden move, he gathered her as he stood. "*Bueno.* When in Rome…"

"What?" she prompted as he carried her into the apartment. "You'll carry me to bed like a concubine?" She could work with that.

"I declare us married."

"You're not the king. Do you really think it will stick?"

"I do." He came down on the bed with her, then lifted his head. "I love you."

His expression reflected the vast feelings contained behind the visage, all darks and lights, fears and ferocities and love. Endless, true-as-gold *love*.

Her heart had always been his, but in that moment she released it to him, freely and without reservation, confident he would protect it with everything in him.

"I love you, too."

Even though he had known she loved him for what must have felt like centuries, his face spasmed with emotion. He closed his eyes as though savoring the words.

"And?" he prompted quietly.

Bossy, bossy man.

Resisting the urge to roll her eyes, because this was very serious and very real, she said very sincerely, "I do."

EPILOGUE

ISIDORA WAS WEARING only a black bra, underpants and garters when Ramon walked into their bedroom.

He came up short, green eyes searing her to the spot as he took her in.

Heart skipping with instant reaction, she playfully ticktocked her hips as she walked across and stepped into the shoes she'd chosen to go with her dress. They were erotically tall with a hint of bondage in the thick black ankle straps. She slanted him a sultry look over her shoulder.

"You approve?"

"Hell, yes. Now I really don't want to go out tonight."

"Oh." She pivoted to face him. One of Paris's hottest new nightclubs was having a grand reopening and they were one of the "it" couples always begged to show up at such events. "Why not?"

He swore under his breath. "I didn't mean that to sound— Of course I want to take you dancing. It's your birthday. I've even gone shopping. That's why I'm late." He brought across a small box of indigo velvet embossed in silver.

She opened the box and caught her breath, dazzled by the earrings. "Spoiler!" She went on tiptoe to kiss him.

His arm went around her, possessive and edging toward dominant as he clasped her close. His kiss was thorough and hot, deeply passionate, leaving her breathless when they finally came up for air.

"Trying to convince me to stay in? I'm listening." She leaned into him, enamored as ever, and let her fingers begin to work on his tie.

But something in the way his mouth flexed into a tight line made her sober.

"What's wrong?" She tried to draw back so she could see him better.

"Nothing." He held on to her. His familiar expression, usually so readable, was disconcertingly cautious. "Absolutely nothing is wrong. I'm being...impatient."

"About what? Did I do something?" Her heart lurched. Their marriage was everything she had ever wished it to be and more. They always seemed to be on the same wavelength, even managing to continue working together despite both having demanding schedules. To hear something was off threw her back into old insecurity.

"Everything you do is perfect. I'm the one." He released her and shrugged out of his suit jacket. "I told myself I would wait until you turned twenty-five and this morning, it was all I could do to let you sleep in without saying something."

"About what?" He had made love to her before he left for the office, telling her to enjoy her day off, and promised to take her out to celebrate tonight. She had drifted off blissfully, thinking she really was living happily ever after. "Ramon, you're scaring me!"

"*I'm* scared. But I still want to do it. I want to have a baby, Isidora."

It took a moment for the words to penetrate, for the meaning to sink in. For her to believe he had actually said them.

"What do you think?" he prompted, watching her closely.

She thought he had just given her the best birthday gift ever. Pushing her knuckles against her lips, she tried to keep them from trembling while a bubble of joy pressed for release in her throat. Her whole chest was expanding, putting an excited sting of moisture into her eyes.

"I don't know how to read this silence." His brows lowered with concern as he came closer. "I know it will be hard. Parenting is hard already without that." He pushed his splayed hand toward the window, where the outside world was always a pressure on his family. Then he took her hand from her mouth and pressed it to his own. "Having you is enough, Isidora. I love you with everything in me. If you think raising a baby in our circus is too much risk, that's okay. But I've been thinking about it for months and had to ask."

"Why on earth did you think you had to wait until I was twenty-five?" Her voice came out as strained and unsteady as she felt. Her legs were so weak, she wobbled in her heels.

"Because you're that much younger than me. And we're not a normal family. You needed time to get used to being a Sauveterre. It's a big ask, Isidora. I know that."

"But I love you. Of course I want your baby. I have since…" She shrugged, not the least self-conscious anymore about the way she had idolized him as a child. That love was mature and real now. Strong and eternal on both sides. "Forever."

He frowned. "Why didn't *you* say something?"

"Because it's a big ask." She slid her arms around his neck, warming her near nude body against his clothed one, loving how he wrapped his arms around her in response, always welcoming her into closeness against him.

"It's been nice having you to myself, being auntie and uncle, running around to see everyone else's children on a whim. Having *you* is enough for me. But if you want a baby? *Yes, please.*"

"You're sure? There's a decent chance it'll be twins," he said dryly.

"Even better."

"You say that now..." He picked her up and she clasped her legs around his waist as he took her toward the bed.

Ten months later, they had a gorgeous little boy with dark hair and green eyes, the spitting of his father and uncle. Two years after that, however, girls arrived with identical auburn locks and gray eyes. Their father shook his head in wry delight.

* * * * *

If you enjoyed
BOUND BY THE MILLIONAIRE'S RING,
why not explore the first two parts of
Dani Collins's
THE SAUVETERRE SIBLINGS *trilogy?*

PURSUED BY THE DESERT PRINCE
HIS MISTRESS WITH TWO SECRETS
Available now!

MILLS & BOON®

EXCLUSIVE EXTRACT

When chauffeur Keira Ryan drives into a snowdrift, she and her devastatingly attractive passenger must find a hotel…but there's only one bed! Luckily Matteo Valenti knows how to make the best of a bad situation—with the most sizzling experience of her life. It's nearly Christmas again before Matteo uncovers Keira's secret. He's avoided commitment his whole life, but now it's time to claim his heir…

Read on for a sneak preview of Sharon Kendrick's book
THE ITALIAN'S CHRISTMAS SECRET
One Night With Consequences

'Santino?' Matteo repeated, wondering if he'd misheard her. He stared at her, his brow creased in a frown. 'You gave him an Italian name?'

'Yes.'

'Why?'

'Because when I looked at him…' Keira's voice faltered as she scraped her fingers back through her hair and turned those big sapphire eyes on him '…I knew I could call him nothing else but an Italian name.'

'Even though you sought to deny him his heritage and kept his birth hidden from me?'

She swallowed. 'You made it very clear that you never wanted to see me again, Matteo.'

His voice grew hard. 'I haven't come here to argue the rights and wrongs of your secrecy. I've come to see my son.'

It was a demand Keira couldn't ignore. She'd seen the brief tightening of his face when she'd mentioned his child and another wave of guilt had washed over her.

'Come with me,' she said huskily.

He followed her up the narrow staircase and Keira was

acutely aware of his presence behind her. She could detect the heat from his body and the subtle sandalwood which was all his and, stupidly, she remembered the way that scent had clung to her skin the morning after he'd made love to her. Her heart was thundering by the time they reached the box-room she shared with Santino and she held her breath as Matteo stood frozen for a moment before moving soundlessly towards the crib.

'Matteo?' she said.

Matteo didn't answer. Not then. He wasn't sure he trusted himself to speak because his thoughts were in such disarray. He stared down at the dark fringe of eyelashes which curved on the infant's olive-hued cheeks and the shock of black hair. Tiny hands were curled into two tiny fists and he found himself leaning forward to count all the fingers, nodding his head with satisfaction as he registered each one.

He swallowed.

His *son*.

He opened his mouth to speak but Santino chose that moment to start to whimper and Keira bent over the crib to scoop him up. 'Would you...would you like to hold him?'

'Not now,' he said abruptly. 'There isn't time. You need to pack your things while I call ahead and prepare for your arrival in Italy.'

'What?'

'You heard me. You can't put out a call for help and then ignore help when it comes. You telephoned me and now you must accept the consequences,' he added grimly.

Don't miss
THE ITALIAN'S CHRISTMAS SECRET
By Sharon Kendrick

Available November 2017

www.millsandboon.co.uk

MILLS & BOON®

Why shop at millsandboon.co.uk?

Each year, thousands of romance readers
find their perfect read at millsandboon.co.uk.
That's because we're passionate about
bringing you the very best romantic fiction.
Here are some of the advantages of
shopping at www.millsandboon.co.uk:

* **Get new books first**—you'll be able to buy
  your favourite books one month before they
  hit the shops

* **Get exclusive discounts**—you'll also be
  able to buy our specially created monthly
  collections, with up to 50% off the RRP

* **Find your favourite authors**—latest news,
  interviews and new releases for all your
  favourite authors and series on our website,
  plus ideas for what to try next

* **Join in**—once you've bought your favourite
  books, don't forget to register with us to rate,
  review and join in the discussions

Visit **www.millsandboon.co.uk**
for all this and more today!

Join Britain's BIGGEST Romance Book Club

50% OFF your first parcel

- **EXCLUSIVE offers** every month

- **FREE delivery direct** to your door

- **NEVER MISS a title**

- **EARN Bonus Book** points

Call Customer Services
0844 844 1358*

or visit
millsandboon.co.uk/subscription